INTEL

A WAYPOINT PREQUEL NOVELLA

DEBORAH ADAMS &
KIMBERLEY PERKINS

eBook ISBN: 978-1-7325071-3-5
Print ISBN: 978-1-3868925-5-7

This book is a work of fiction. Any references to historical events, real people, or real places are used fictitiously. Other names, characters, places and events are products of the author's imagination, and any resemblances to actual events or places or persons, living or dead, is entirely coincidental.

Edited by Kristen Tate, The Blue Garret.
Published in the United States of America.
First edition 2018.

Rocket City Publishing
990 Explorer Blvd. NW
Huntsville, AL 35806

CONTENTS

1

QUINN LEHI WAS GOOD at getting information. Her methods were not always what some would consider ethical, but they were effective. For instance, there was the means by which she'd landed this internship. Most people would assume it had to do with her mother. They would be wrong. She'd been accepted into the intern class of 2067 at the United Nations Investigation Department, and she'd done it without the support of her mom.

That same mother currently stood at the door, arms crossed and foot tapping. "Hurry up. You can't be late for your first day."

Quinn grabbed a muffin from the counter and slung a duffel bag over her shoulder. Her mom's critical gaze slid over her rumpled gym clothes. She didn't look pleased.

"Could you have tried any less to impress today?"

Quinn assessed herself. It was her typical workout gear. Fitted black calf-length pants, tennis shoes, and a slouchy tee she could never quite keep on both shoulders at once. It was practical. Comfortable.

"The letter from the Intel Chief said field wear. We have to complete our physicals first."

Her mother's lips drew tight, but she didn't say anything else. She simply opened the door and walked through, expecting Quinn to follow, which she did; Agent Karyn Lehi was not a woman you wanted to cross. Quinn drew some comfort in knowing she wasn't the only one.

At the agency, her mom was a legend. She'd been promoted to director less than a year ago. Quinn looked a lot like her, but she couldn't help thinking everything that made her mom spectacular was muted in her own features. Her mother's Japanese heritage was present in both of them, but where her mother had porcelain skin, Quinn's was marred with freckles. And while she had her mother's soulful, dark, almond-shaped eyes, what she saw in the mirror seemed less vivid than what she saw when she held her mother's gaze.

Agent Lehi was never-a-hair-out-of-place perfect at all times. Her suit fit like she was born to it, and even when she was dressed in tactical gear, she made it look elegant. Whereas Quinn's style was forever a disappointment.

Quinn also didn't have quite the same edge as her mother because, you know, Quinn smiled on occasion. She was actually a bit of a softy. She loved a good romcom, and blood made her queasy. But there had to be more than one way to be a good agent. It had been the only thing she'd wanted to do since the first time she'd walked through the giant double doors of UNID headquarters for a school field trip in the fourth grade. Their tour guide, a bubbly intern with more enthusiasm than seemed healthy, sparked her first moment of *yes, this is everything I need* with just one sentence: "This building is where all the information in the world is kept."

At that age, she couldn't fathom an entire world of information at her fingertips. Once she got a little older, she'd figured out ways to make that happen from the comfort of her own home, but she'd always had a drive to *know* things. Maybe it was a byproduct of her mother's decision to never tell her anything. She'd had to investigate the identity of her own father, for heaven's sake!

"Navigate to work," her mom said, shutting the door of their sedan. "When was the last time you visited the gym?" she asked as they settled into the spacious back seat and their car slid out of the driveway.

Quinn had to think hard about that one. "I don't know, sometime last week."

Her mom's sigh was heavy. "You knew the physical was on your first day, and you haven't been conditioning?"

"I'm interning for a desk intel job, not field work. It's an insignificant part of the position, and I'll still exceed minimum standards."

"That's your goal? Exceed minimum standards?" Her mother's gaze grew fierce. "I thought you wanted this job."

"I do! I've been spending extra time in my lab. Last night I finished building an algorithm that should patch into the agency facial rec software to test variations based on common concealment techniques. I got the idea from one of my class projects last semester."

"What are some of the concealment methods you accounted for?"

Quinn was taken aback. Her mom never showed interest in her projects. She expected perfect grades, but she rarely wanted details.

"Well, facial hair and eye wear, of course, and it will sometimes manage detection through small surgical procedures like cheek implants."

"That's good. I hope it works when you need it."

It was a compliment. From her mother. She decided to take it as a sign that today was going to be a good day. She was going to rock this internship.

THIS WAS BAD. VERY, *very bad*, she thought as she bent over, hands on knees, and lungs burning for oxygen. As it turned out, the first day of physicals were combined for all the interns. Meaning they were lumped in with the field agent hopefuls, and the commander in charge of field agent interns thought minimum standards were for "weaklings," and UNID didn't need weaklings.

She wondered if her mom had any part in this guy's training at some point.

She'd thought there would at least be some form of camaraderie amongst her fellow deskers—but no. Their icy stares had disabused her of that notion from the moment she'd walked into the squad room.

She was competition, and it was every rookie for themselves. She was now lagging at the back of the pack and seriously considering her life choices.

She glanced about for anyone who might be struggling as much as she was, but her team had become nothing more than obscure blobs in the distance.

Her morning had been one long series of mishaps. She'd shown up in her slouchy exercise clothes only to find that every other intern had dressed for the Olympics. Surrounded by well-groomed twenty-year-olds in their fitted high-performance gear, she'd felt frumpy in comparison. Then she'd made the ultimate mistake of falling on her sixteenth pushup and making the entire group start over. Understandably, they now hated her.

"Lehi! Move it! This isn't window shopping with your girlfriends."

She set out again with the slowest pace she could manage and still look like she was jogging. Her long legs usually ate up the pavement but not for this long. She needed a distraction, so she blocked out the pain in her side and focused on her team.

She'd learned everything there was to dig up about them in the week since she'd discovered their identities. There were six of them total, including Quinn. Three women and three men all between the ages of twenty and twenty-two.

She was only two months older than the youngest, Elena Petrova. Elena was crazy smart. She'd finished top of her class two years early. Quinn had actually tried reaching out to the guy who'd come in second, just to see if he knew any weaknesses she might have, but he'd mumbled something nervously that she couldn't understand and hung up abruptly. Needless to say, Elena already scared the crap out of her.

While not quite as scary, the other interns were similarly impressive on paper, but no more than Quinn. Each had their own special set of skills and merits. Elena Petrova, chemical engineering; Gretchen De Vries, ballistics; Finlay Evans, linguistics; Oliver Lee, forensic accounting, and Luan Pillay, data analysis. While her own specialty was algorithm development, she could hold her own in all their swim lanes.

By the time she caught up to the rest of the group, at the end of the most grueling run she'd ever experienced, it was to find that the water was gone. No one looked like they felt any sympathy. In fact, Gretchen looked openly smug as Quinn cast a sorrowful glance at the empty water container and crumpled paper cups littering the beverage table.

The commander surveyed the group. "It's obvious that many of you have been working hard to stay in prime physical condition, and some of you"—Quinn swore he looked directly into her junk food junkie soul with his concentrated stare—"have been lazy as hell. Maybe you think that you're so smart and special it doesn't matter. I'm here to tell you that you are mistaken."

Quinn felt a knotty lump settle at the bottom of her stomach. The longer he talked, the more confident she was that she would never make it. His requirements were so far beyond anything she would be able to master in the few months of this program.

She heard a small shuffling sound as someone inched up just behind her. "Hey, it's Lehi, right?" Elena whispered, her Russian accent faint but recognizable.

Quinn nodded.

"Why didn't we see you in the dorms last night? Everyone was here except you."

"I'm...local," she whispered, thinking furiously. She'd figured the dorms were unnecessary. She lived here. But she hadn't considered that as the other interns were from all over the world, they'd be housed at UNID together. She was probably going to miss a lot by not being there in their off hours. Her mind was made up in a second. "I'm moving in today. No need to be here before we even started." She'd barely moved her mouth, attempting to reply as covertly as possible, but of course their torturer still managed to notice.

"Is there something you'd like to share with all of us, Lehi? I sincerely hope you are under no illusions that your name in UNID will get you anywhere unless you can prove yourself on your own merits. The Director has made it clear you get no special treatment. You understand that, right?"

All eyes turned to her. Maybe they hadn't heard him shouting her name when she was at the back of the pack and beyond hearing distance, but they noticed it now, and it appeared they had made the connection. Several eyebrows lifted in her direction. What had been tired faces moments before became downright hostile. *Great.*

She nodded her head and kept her mouth shut as embarrassment heated her face more than the punishing run had.

"Glad to hear it. Alright, everyone hit the showers and meet in the lobby in forty-five minutes. Dismissed."

People quickly made their way across the training field and toward the dorm showers. The dorms were a newer addition to the UNID complex. Before they were built, there was just a floor in HQ dedicated to housing off-duty agents and a special section for visiting dignitaries trying to stay under the radar. Apparently, the dignitaries had felt uneasy about having agents underfoot coming and going from the posh apartments, so the whole floor had been turned over to visitors and their personal security, and the dorms were built for agents.

The narrow dorms fell under the shadow of the headquarters building. It was a massive steel and marble pillar just a couple blocks from the UN capitol building. Proximity made it easier to coordinate security and investigations with the president and his staff.

Reaching beneath a bench at the edge of the field, Quinn grabbed the bag she'd brought with a change of clothes while whispers drifted in her direction from the other deskers, behind her.

"Let me get this straight, there's only one slot, and we're up against the director's family?" That question was posed by Oliver.

She tried to keep walking and pretend she couldn't hear them. If she could just move faster, she might have been able to accomplish it, but her legs were still jelly from the run.

"Not just family," Elena's voice came louder than Oliver's—were they getting closer? "She's her daughter."

Quinn's head snapped around. All five of the other deskers, huddled only twenty yards away around a data-pad, looked up at her as one. She'd heard that expression, "if looks could kill," but it always seemed like a fairly melodramatic thing to say. Now? She got it. Because if a look could cause physical harm, she'd be a pile of ashes blowing in the breeze.

She turned stiffly back in the direction of the showers. Focus. She needed to focus. Their opinions meant nothing; they'd all be gone once she won the position anyway. The drill sergeant, whose name had escaped her, would not take it easy on her. So what? She didn't want easy. She needed to earn this. Could her mom not have alerted everyone to her presence? Could she not have made it harder for her? Sure, but that would probably require an alien takeover of her mom's mind and body, and something about being constantly judged and scrutinized just felt like home.

She took the fastest shower she'd ever taken, also using it as an opportunity to gulp down water. The other girls in the women's wash room were quiet, everyone keeping to their own thoughts, which she was grateful for. She didn't have the energy for confrontations.

Pulling out the skirt, blouse, and blazer she'd pressed and packed for the day, she was mildly alarmed at the wrinkled state of her shirt. She should have had it hanging, not folded into a canvas bag. *Why do you never think of these things ahead of time?* Karyn Lehi's voice was very clear in her head.

She dressed in the less than pristine ensemble and low black pumps her mom had given her for her twentieth birthday a few months ago.

Staring at herself in the full-length mirror, she pulled her damp hair back into a low ponytail and considered her reflection. It was not a disaster. In fact, despite her slightly rumpled blouse, she looked quite nice. Professional.

That was when Elena and Gretchen stepped up to the counter by the sinks to touch up their makeup. Both women were wearing perfectly fitted designer suits, complete with heels Quinn would break her ankles in. Her look, in comparison, had her feeling like a pre-pubescent teen next to supermodels. And Elena was younger than she was! How did she manage to look more sophisticated? Was it a Russian thing?

Didn't matter now. They threw her condescending looks she was sure were meant to intimidate. It worked. She was totally intimidated. Nothing had gone right today, and now she looked like a child next to the other contenders.

Squaring her shoulders, she tried to push away self-doubt. Once she got her fingers on a keypad, everything would turn around.

Everyone was gathered in the lobby a short while later, but no one was talking. Oliver leaned against a white marble wall, looking especially disinterested in everything and everyone. An adorably rumpled Finlay managed to bustle in right as the drill sergeant and another, even beefier, man stepped up to address them.

"Alright, children," said the beefy man in his tight black UNID T-shirt, crossing his arms and looking nearly as disinterested as Oliver.

Quinn barely restrained an eye roll. Children?

"Agent Bleakly will be overseeing the Field Agent hopefuls, and the Intel Specialists will come with me." *Bleakly?* Honestly, she'd never met a man so aptly named.

The fieldies followed Bleakly to the right-hand stairwell while the deskers took off after—had he even said his name? What was with these guys and not introducing themselves? It was hardly polite.

She'd only taken a couple of steps before she was knocked to the side by a hard shoulder on her left. She was slightly stunned to see Gretchen saunter past without a backward glance. Quinn looked around. Did no one else see that? But the group just filed after their leader. With a sigh she caught up to the back of the pack. "Children" was right.

2

TURNED OUT THEIR MASSIVE babysitter's name was Agent Hart. His arms were so big that they couldn't rest comfortably at his sides, and he hadn't cracked a smile since he had told them to follow him. Her team trailed behind him like obedient kindergarteners as he led them through the maze of corridors of UNID headquarters.

They all crammed into an elevator, and Quinn lifted an eyebrow when Hart selected the basement level. She guessed newbies had to start in the dungeons.

She had expected her team's setup to be a conference room table and a few laptops but was giddy with surprise. The intern office was three floors down from the big-girl intelligence office, but it still looked like a scaled-back version of the real command and control, where certified intelligence agents were always tapping away on their glowing screens and bustling around with new discoveries. *That* was what she wanted one day, what she'd worked so hard for, but this would do for now.

There was a terminal for each of them, with raised partitions in between stations. The surfaces of her desk and the walls were glowing with screens that were ready for her commands. There were panels with brightly colored switches and buttons. She didn't know what any of them did, but she would find out.

She grinned brightly, a sense of belonging flooding into her and radiating warmth through to her fingertips. Quinn knew that *this* was where she was meant to be.

She took the empty terminal between Elena and Finlay and spun in her seat for a moment, taking in the office. So what if she'd done less than extraordinarily during the physical. With her hands on the keys, she was in her element—tapped in and ready to go.

"Hi, I'm Finlay, but cute ladies like yourself can call me Finn," said the boy next door—um, next station, over. Wearing a grin full of mischief, he held out his hand. She grasped it firmly, trying to ignore the hint of electricity that raced up her arm. *He might be one of the biggest perks of this program.*

"Just call me Quinn," she said, returning his grin.

"Yikes," he said, "Quinn and Finn? If they call roll for this thing we might have to separate."

She coughed out a laugh and turned back to her station, trying to hide how much she enjoyed his teasing. She'd barely fiddled with the widgets that decorated her high-tech station when the door to her new office whished open and the familiar tap of sensible shoes made her whirl around at attention.

Karyn Lehi didn't need to introduce herself. Quinn had seen it play out many times in her life. People knew to follow her mother, knew to go silent so they could hear her orders. The murmur of the interns came to a halt, and Agent Hart barreled out of his chair, his hulking form going rigid in the presence of his superior officer.

There were no pleasantries, no how-are-yous, and not one single glance in Quinn's direction. "A high-profile item was stolen from Crystal City Bank this morning. I figured this would be a nice bit of fodder for our rookies, Hart."

"Of course, ma'am. Where are we?" the beefy agent asked.

"We have boots on the ground, eyes in the sky, and C-SIGs ready for deployment. Details are on the sharedrive." The words came out of her mouth flatly, with an air of boredom.

"We're on it, Director Lehi," Hart said.

Her mother turned toward the door but paused before exiting. "You have a day until we send this out to the real intelligence officers and let them handle it." Her eyes cut to Quinn for a brief second, and

Quinn felt her stomach drop. "Catch the culprits who robbed Crystal City Bank and prove you're worthy of this internship, or else we'll find six more rookies to take your places."

"Yes, ma'am," some of the other cadets answered, but Quinn was silent.

She could feel a migraine settling in as she glared openly at her mother's retreating back. Did she think she was going to scare Quinn out of this internship? That she wouldn't be able to handle it? She would prove her wrong.

No one was taking this job from her. She'd claw her way to the top of the pack and get the coveted intel specialist position if it was the last thing she did, and not even Director Karyn Lehi could stop her.

"Let's get to work, kids!" A thunderclap echoed when Agent Hart smacked his massive hands together. "You can access the sharedrive by tapping on—"

Quinn didn't hear the rest. She'd already blocked the clatter of noise in the room out and swiveled in her chair to her screens. Her long black ponytail lagged behind her, cutting a swath through the air like a whip.

She pulled up the crime scene files quickly and started reading. There wasn't a whole lot to go on, but the amount that they had was a testament to the efficiency of UNID. Two hours before, the manager of Crystal City Bank had arrived for his morning shift and discovered that the vault door to the safety deposit boxes had been blown off its hinges and over a dozen boxes had been emptied.

The boxes were not in the same location, nor did they appear to be chosen at random. It was as if the robbers had knowledge of the contents of the vault. They had pulled only the boxes that had the most expensive items inside.

One item in particular had escalated this case up to UNID's jurisdiction: the Starlight Diamond. It was one of the only remaining large diamonds in the world, weighing in at 529.3 carats. Long ago, many gems across the globe could claim heftier sizes, but rich families had slowly broken heirlooms apart during inheritance proceedings. The Starlight Diamond arguably belonged in a museum, but its owner, Helga Wilhelminer, had locked it up from prying eyes many years before.

One of the most beautiful gems in the world hadn't seen the light of day in decades, and now it was missing.

The ballistics report on the vault door revealed that the heist was performed yesterday evening, a few hours after the bank had closed for the night.

The first boots on the ground had not reported any evidence of a breach into the building. In fact, the bank's security system was constantly monitored by police, and entry into the building during nonwork hours was restricted to a few select employees. Security measures were also heightened during the off hours, and they included retinal scans, hand geometry scans, and voice recognition.

The lack of forced entry and the items taken suggested that it was an inside job, but all of the bank's upper management who would have had access to the building and the safety deposit manifest had solid alibis. At the time of the robbery, all of the employees with access were at the White House celebrating President Camden's successful power grid project. In fact, at the time in question, the *Globe Daily* had snapped a photo of the bank's upper management and posted it to their feed.

The security system also showed no door entry timestamped between the time the last employee left for the day and the manager arrived.

The robbers were ghosts, and they had a little over a twelve-hour head start on the investigation team. Quinn's dream job depended on her finding, by close of business today, a criminal that had seemingly vanished into thin air. If she couldn't, she would be under her mother's control for longer than she wanted, and her whole team of interns would lose any chance of continuing forward with the selection process.

It was time to forget they were competitors and work as a unit.

However, that was going to be easier said than done because Elena Petrova had come to the same conclusion and had already appointed herself the lead on the investigation.

And Elena Petrova was a nightmare. She was one of those women that intimidated every man, woman, and child she came in contact with. She was fierce and opinionated, with features so striking and beautiful that she seemed unreal. Her eyes were an icy blue that was near white, and her hair was a rich brown and placed in a flawless bun atop her head.

Quinn buttoned her blazer to look a little more put together

"We need to direct the team on the ground to inspect the blast more thoroughly. If we can identify the chemicals used to blow it, then we can trace it back to the source." Elena ordered Oliver to get on the line with UNID's ground force.

"Seems like a swell start," Finn said, long legs stretched in front of him and crossed at the ankle.

"The chemicals are in the forensic examiner's report. They blew it with a common plastic explosive, formed into a shape charge to help control the blast. Simple and rudimentary. And all anyone has done this morning is dig through the blast. If there was anything to find, someone would have found it by now," Quinn said, crossing her arms.

"I'm sure you don't know, but the smallest variation in the recipe could be a clue that would break this case wide open. I studied under Anatoly Mikhailov for two years—"

Quinn waved her hand dismissively. She would not be bullied into following a theory that the ground team had already been working for hours. "We should branch out and explore the rest of the crime scene. Deploy the bots—"

"There's a whole team of investigators on site," Oliver said, swiveling toward them. "The bots will just get in their way. Besides, they will write up reports of their findings. It's more efficient if we just follow up on their leads."

"Elena's idea could work. We're all on the line here," Gretchen said, already pulling up known terrorist factions' chemical formulas.

"I'm sure they aren't going to kick Quinn *Lehi* out of here on her first day," Elena snapped. "Get to work, everyone. Don't let her distract you."

Quinn's mouth dropped open. She was in the same boat as all of them. Her mother being the director meant nothing. In fact, it meant less. Kathryn Lehi didn't want her there, so Quinn had to work twice as hard to prove herself.

Before she could jump in, Finn chimed back, "No reason we can't pursue multiple avenues. Quinn and I will investigate the scene with the bots; you guys look into the chemical signatures. Let's just make it through the day." His accent was thick with sophistication and English charm.

Elena didn't turn from her terminal; she just shrugged and kept working.

Quinn noticed Agent Hart scribble something in a notebook.

"I've never driven a robot before," Finn said, a lazy smile splitting his face as he walked his rolling chair over to hers.

She was happy she was sitting down because a smile like that could knock a girl off her feet. But there was no time for swooning. There was work to be done, and a mystery to solve.

The C-SIG units were designed so intelligence personnel didn't have to waste time traveling to crime scenes. The bots, referred to as golems by UNID staff, could be controlled virtually from a terminal, take samples and analyze them inside their housing, and sweep across a crime scene without disturbing any evidence.

That is, if you knew how to fly one. It had become very apparent to her three seconds into the deployment that Finn did not, in fact, know how to control a C-SIG unit. He could barely get it off the ground. The sad smile that Finn had sported was enough for her to ignore his shortcoming. She had suggested that they explore the scene using only one golem.

All of the interns worked through lunch without taking a break. She tried to ignore the ah-has that echoed across the office, and instead focused on her own leads. From her golem's vantage point above the crime scene, she could see the ground team swarming the blast area and gathering up clues inside the vault. She had a live feed of their discoveries popping up on one of her monitors, and had Finn reading it aloud to her as she piloted their bot. Every time an on-site investigator sent in a report to HQ, a ding would sound, and Finn would read it to her.

The subject matter was all cold hard science, but his voice was velvety and distracting. She steered the bot away from the blast area and flew around the perimeter of the building.

The biggest mystery about this case wasn't that the vault door had been breached, and it wasn't that they had stolen one of the biggest diamonds in the world. It was that whoever had done it had vanished without a trace. The security system was thorough. All exits were covered with motion detection, including the air system. All doors required biometric scans that were as solid as UNIDs internal system.

How had they escaped?

Her eye twitched when the other team of interns got a lead and were loudly bragging to one another.

She noticed the worried look on Finn's face out of the corner of her eye and felt guilty. He broke from the pack to be on her team, and she was failing.

"Do you think we should consolidate our efforts now, Quinn?" Finn whispered to her.

"I need to know how they got out. If you want to jump in with them—"

"No, no, it's fine. We'll continue onward, fearless leader," Finn said with a warm smile. The terminal dinged, and his eyes darted to a new posting that had appeared in the feed. "Looks like the on-site investigators finished their sweep for trace evidence. No fingerprints that shouldn't have been there. No physical evidence to go on. I'm sure the soot from the explosion isn't helping."

A glance at the clock told her that she only had two hours to track down this diamond. Even if Elena's theory panned out, the robbers could be halfway across the country by now. They needed to apprehend them and secure the gemstone before her mother returned, or they were all toast.

Once more the terminal dinged, but this time Finn said nothing.

"What was that?" Quinn asked, eyes burning as she focused on navigating the C-SIG through the ventilation ducts.

"They are just putting their package together. It's the blueprints of the building," Finn said.

"Pull them up. I want to see them." Quinn piloted the bot out of the vent cover she had removed and landed it skillfully on a teller's desk.

Finn tapped on the glass of her terminal and the blueprints flooded the screens. Quinn leaned back in her chair and studied the schematics.

"What do you mean it's a dead end?" Elena shrieked at the other interns. "We identified the chemical agent. That should be enough to find them."

"It's from a manufacturer of demolition materials in Maine. They had a break-in six months ago. They never found out who did it," Oliver said.

"This is unacceptable," Elena hissed back.

"There's nothing we can do. Those are the facts," Gretchen said.

"We're running out of time. Director Lehi is going to fire all of us on our first day." Oliver had lost his cool and was flat-out panicking.

Quinn really wished they would calm down. Sure, their time was running out, but having an anxiety attack wasn't going to make anything better. Then again, the rest of the team didn't have the most charming Englishman on this side of the Atlantic whispering reassurances in their ears.

It was 4:45. Her mother would be here any second. She was probably clicking her sensible shoes down the hall, a smile on her face at the possibility of firing six people on their first day.

Just when the room reached its crescendo of panic, just when it seemed like six other cadets would replace them in the program, Quinn saw it in the blueprints.

She fired up the electric engine on her golem and whirled the bot around in the air, darting for the blast area.

No wonder no one noticed. The area was covered in soot and shrapnel. No one would have noticed that the short corridor to the vault that should have been seven feet wide was only five and a half.

"Call the ground team and tell them I need a team in position with guns drawn in two minutes," Quinn said to Finn.

He grabbed her desk phone, repeating her orders as she flew her C-SIG up to the wall and looked for a seam. It hadn't been damaged by the explosion but had been covered in blackened soot. Concealed in the ashes was a hairline split.

The door whooshed open, and then she heard her mother say, "Time's up, cadets."

Her hands didn't leave the controls. The boots of the ground team settled in behind her bot, and Quinn used it to pull at the drywall much like she had done earlier with the vent cover.

And there they were—two idiots that had hidden in the walls of the bank, twenty-five feet from where they had stolen one of the largest diamonds on Earth. The UNID agents at Crystal City Bank had them handcuffed and in the back of a squad car in no time. It didn't take long to figure out how they'd done it. The bank had been revamped earlier in the year, and these two knuckleheads had been on the crew. The bank's layout had shifted to accommodate a larger vault, which must have made the false wall harder for the employees to spot.

"We did it!" Finn yipped. He gave her a high five and flashed a lovely smile at her.

"Well done, team," her mother said, with an air of approval that Quinn had rarely experienced in her life.

Agent Hart slapped her on the back for a job well done, and Quinn nearly fell out of her swivel chair from the force of it. With his babysitting duties done for the day, he left shortly after.

The fuzzy feeling that always came along with solving a mystery made her feel like she was floating.

She grabbed her gym bag and purse from under her terminal and turned to the rest of the cadets. "Looks like we live to fight another day," Quinn said, smiling at the team.

Elena snorted. "You know, I was top of my class at the academy. I scored two prestigious apprenticeships. That's what it took for *me* to get here." Her voice was venomous. "What did you put on your application? Special skills: Lehi's daughter."

"I—"

"See you tomorrow, Lehi." With that, Elena stomped out of the room.

The other three cadets that had been on the losing team gave her similar looks of contempt before making their exits. She'd just saved their jobs and not one of them was grateful.

"They'll come around," Finn said, grabbing his bag off the back of his chair. "And if they don't, who cares? We both know that the underdogs won out today."

"Would you have been that petulant if their theory had been right and we had lost?"

"Never would have happened, Q," Finn said, his easy smile unwavering. "I never lose."

She smiled, happy that she'd met Finn, and that she had someone on her side.

Then she thought about what Elena had asked her.

What did Quinn put on her application to the cadet program?

Her father's last name.

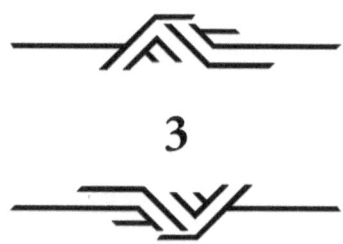

3

QUINN SURREPTITIOUSLY made her way to her mom's office. She'd wanted to avoid this, but she needed her stuff from home if she was going to live with this nest of vipers.

Knocking on the cool metal door, she waited to be allowed through.

"Yes, come in."

Upon entering, she shut the door quickly behind her. She didn't want people to see them together more than absolutely necessary.

Her mom looked up from the neat stack of papers on her desk. No doubt, some of the most important correspondence in the world was right in front of her. Quinn couldn't help a twinge of longing to snoop that raced up her spine. The hard look on her mom's face squashed it though.

"I'd prefer if you didn't visit me here, Quinn."

"Yes, Director, I understand," she said with barely repressed sarcasm, "but I need a favor. I've decided to stay in the dorms with the other interns. Could you pack a bag when you get home and send it back in the car?"

"Director, is it?" her mom said with a faint grin, leaning back in her chair.

"I can keep it professional," Quinn replied, smoothing her hands over the gray pencil skirt and praying the low lights in her office hid any imperfections.

"You did good work today. Though, I hear it didn't start out quite as well as it ended."

The wry comment nearly made her wince. Considering the stiffness in her limbs, she'd be feeling this morning's butt kicking for days to come.

"I may have been less prepared than I thought I was," she replied diplomatically.

"If you want to take this seriously, you'll need to be either the best or one of the best in every area, and I'm not just talking about exercise. We both know your hand-to-hand combat skills are inadequate."

Quinn's breath lodged in her throat. "The application package didn't say anything about—"

"It's a new requirement, and while you didn't have to come into the program with fighting skills, all of the interns will be expected to cultivate them."

"But that's ridiculous! We're deskers," she all but shouted.

"This conversation is over. Adapt or go home. Do you still want a bag packed?" she asked as she stood to pick up her briefcase and put away the documents she'd been reading.

Quinn bit her tongue to stop more words from spilling out before nodding.

"Very well. I should be able to have it here in an hour. Goodnight." With that parting statement, her mother pointed Quinn out the door.

She slumped back to the elevators with much less confidence than she'd come up with. How did her mother manage to do that to her every time?

She'd taken karate for two years when she was in middle school, and it had been painfully obvious she had no aptitude for it. The one tournament where she had actually got in a good, solid strike on her opponent, she'd nearly thrown up. She would relive the sound of the girl's broken-nosed screams for the rest of her life.

She pressed the button for the first floor. She needed food, and the cafeteria would be serving dinner for another hour at least, so she could just eat and try to come up with a plan for this new development.

She picked up a sandwich from the deli section and sat in a mostly empty dining room. Everyone else must have already eaten.

So, what were her options? Quit or learn to fight.

Her choices sucked. She rolled her head from side to side and tried to relieve the tension that had built in her neck.

She'd promised herself this job. But now they'd gone and changed the rules on her. Had her mom had anything to do with the increased requirements? She didn't want to think her mom had intentionally made this more difficult, but the thought was still there. She'd need to start training immediately—as in tonight. Her weary muscles nearly rebelled from her mind's decision. Could your body mutiny against you?

There was a training room in the building. She'd head there after her bag arrived.

That was that. Decision made and no going back. She'd just have to learn to kick butt, or at least, not have her butt handed to her.

Food finished, she referenced her data-pad to brush up on her karate. After the hour had passed, she walked back to the portico to meet the car. Her mom had packed her things in a press-save bag, which meant she'd not have to worry about wrinkles. *Ever the overachiever, Mom.* She couldn't help but admit it was sometimes handy. She directed the car to drive back home and headed to the locker room of the training center to change.

When she emerged into the training center, she was relieved to at least be in comfortable clothes once again. There were not many people in the room this late. A couple of agents, two guys probably in their late thirties, were sparring in the boxing ring which was prominently positioned in the middle of the large space. A small group of four were weight lifting in the corner, each paired up to spot the respective lifters of the round. Lastly, there was an Indian girl, probably her age, destroying a heavy bag hanging by the side of the ring. This girl was something. Her jabs and kicks were flying so fast it was hard to keep up.

Quinn's original plan had been to work with a heavy bag. But that would mean working out next to this fully competent agent/goddess and embarrassing herself completely. Maybe she could wait her out.

She scanned the room for something else to occupy herself with while she waited for the other girl to wrap it up. The training center was top-of-the-line. It had everything you could need for various forms of fighting styles.

She was taking in some of the more high-tech simulation stations when out of the corner of her eye she saw Elena creeping up the back stairwell heading for the floor above them. *Weird.* She figured she would be the only one still up at this point. That girl was going to make her life here difficult. She could already tell. Then, before she turned away, she saw Oliver dash up right behind Elena.

Were the interns meeting without her? It would completely ruin the purpose of staying here if they still cut her out of things like this.

Anger rose up and spurred her forward. *Hell no.* She dashed in the direction of the stairwell and followed them up. The door to the next floor up was just clicking shut when she rounded the first half landing. She opened the door slowly and peeked inside. It was just a floor of offices and empty Intel terminals. There was a faint light under one of the doors that hadn't shut completely. Creeping up, she could hear voices but couldn't make out the words. Was the whole team here plotting ways to get her cut? She peeked through the crack of light.

Uh—nope. That was not what this was about. There were hands everywhere. They were wrapped so tightly that Quinn couldn't tell where Elena started and Oliver ended.

Yikes! She needed to get out of here unnoticed. Although they were doing a pretty good job of distracting each other. She'd be surprised if either one noted her slight shuffling. She quietly back-stepped one foot then another.

A tap on her shoulder had her body recoiling hard, and her heart nearly somersaulting out of her chest.

She was amazed that she had managed not to scream out loud.

Turning sharply, she met the hard eyes of the girl from the punching bag downstairs. Her arms were crossed, and she held an impatient expression.

She really didn't want Elena and Oliver to find her lurking in the hallway outside their make-out session like a perv. So she took a chance that the girl would understand and lifted a finger to her lips. Her perfectly shaped eyebrows drew together, and she took a step around Quinn to peek inside. Quinn held her breath, praying she wouldn't give her away. When the girl turned back her expression had changed to one of mirth, and Quinn let out a breath of relief. Humor she could manage. Tiptoeing like a pair of bandits, they silently made their way back to the stairwell and let the door softly click behind them.

The girl's soft laughter brought a grin to her own face.

"Who are they, and why aren't they using a more private location for their groping?"

"Well, um—that was Elena Petrova and Oliver Lee. We're interns. When I saw them sneaking up the stairs I had thought the other interns were meeting without me, so I followed. As for why they don't want anyone to know, I'm not sure. Nothing has been as I expected. Everyone is cutthroat competitive."

"Yeah, I remember that part."

"Right, of course. Field agent?"

"What?" she asked with a smirk. "Don't think I could cut it as a desker?"

Quinn grinned. "Sure, but that would be a total waste considering the beating you were delivering to that bag downstairs."

The girl's answering smile lit up her face. "Guess you've got me pegged. I'm Riya Kapoor, by the way."

"Quinn...Lehi," she said, shaking the agent's hand.

Quinn waited for a reaction, but Riya's face remained open and friendly. Maybe one person in this place wouldn't make a big deal about her mother.

Riya began to unwrap the bandaging from her hands as they stepped back into the training center. "Were you getting in some drills too?"

Quinn didn't answer, but Riya must have read the expression on her face.

"What? Sore subject?" Riya asked.

"No—I mean, yes. Hand-to-hand isn't my strong suit."

"I hope that means you're actually going for a desker slot, because if not, you're kinda screwed, Lehi."

"I'm competing for the Intel Specialist job, but they raised the stakes on us and added in combat."

"Yikes, that sucks. But hey, maybe your fellow smarty-pants competitors will be equally unimpressive."

"A girl can hope."

Riya took a quick look at her watch. "Look, I'm about to head out, but I can work with you at the bag for a few minutes if you think it would help."

Quinn would be crazy not to take her up on the offer. She needed the help, and Riya was obviously good at this. But she felt guilty for putting Riya off her planned schedule. She'd figure this out on her own.

"Actually—"

"Nope. Forget I asked. I'm telling you right now to line up with the bag over there."

She stared open-mouthed as Riya refastened her gloves and walked away. She'd completely dismissed Quinn's protest. Not feeling like she had any alternative, she followed.

"What hand are you?" Riya asked.

Quinn shrugged in defeat. "Left."

"Nice, me too," she said with a smile. "Okay, let me see your stance. Lead with your right foot. I just want to see you throw a punch."

And that's how they proceeded for the next half hour. Riya would toss out commands, and Quinn would obey. Things she'd forgotten started to come back to her. Sweat was dripping down her face and between her shoulders by the time Riya called it a night.

"Good work. Maybe tomorrow you won't feel so rusty. You have some good instincts. Trust them, and you'll be fine."

Quinn made her way to her small dorm apartment and collapsed after setting the alarm.

The first day had been a roller coaster. She'd been sure at some moments that she was done for, but her success in finding the jewel thieves was a pinnacle moment. Then, she'd found a friend, which she was only just realizing she had needed badly.

Maybe things were looking up. She wasn't as nervous now about fighting, but Mom had said she needed to be first or second in all the different challenges that the team would face. She knew she could place first in the investigative portion. Physical fitness was obviously her worst, so she'd have to train. If she focused her physical training on her fighting, she might be able to eke out a metaphorical silver medal there, and at least not come in last in fitness. Surely a first in what was obviously the most important aspect, a second in combat, and a not-last in fitness would be enough. Plan in place, she resolved to make it work tomorrow, and fell fast asleep.

4

IT HAD BEEN A WEEK since the program had started, and Quinn was finally settling into her new routine. She would wake up bright and early, so she'd have time for not only breakfast but also making herself look halfway professional. After that, she would try to be the first intern in their office, but after arriving at the earliest she could manage, the ungodly 6 a.m., and still not beating Luan, she'd decided it was a losing battle and conceded.

Living in the dormitories was something she'd wanted to do to fit in—to really give the program her all. But it did come with drawbacks. The dorms were very spartan, with only the basic necessities available. The desk that had been provided wasn't big enough to house the equipment that she kept at home, so she was forced to hustle over to the intern office anytime she needed to work after hours.

That would have been fine. She could have toughed it out, but Elena Petrova was the worst.

How one single person had managed to get on her every last nerve was beyond Quinn's reasoning. It was as if the girl went out of her way to cause her trouble. Elena was always shooting her ideas down during work hours, taking her clothes out of the dryer before they were finished in the shared laundry room, and attributing every accomplishment Quinn had to her mother.

So, it was official. Quinn hated her. She hated her so much that she was openly glaring while she waited for the ribbon cutting ceremony to begin. She was imagining an epic confrontation where she was far more confident than she ever was in real life, and Elena left in tears. Then, a standing ovation would follow from the rest of the agents and maybe a musical number.

The ceremony was for the newly erected monument to commemorate the successful implementation of the Global Power Project, but surely the crowd wouldn't mind if Elena got what was coming to her before the ribbon was cut.

"You look insane right now, Lehi," Riya said. "Now move it. You're blocking the door."

Quinn jumped out of her stupor and shuffled forward to a more open area. Riya trailed behind her, looking out of place in gym clothes. All around them were important people that had come to help President Richard Camden and Vice President Nathan Gamble celebrate the GPP, and at the center of it was Riya, clad in gym shorts that hung below her knees, sneakers, and a loose-fitting tee. Field agents really did live according to different standards than deskers, or maybe it was just Riya. Maybe no one said anything about her wearing gym clothes all over headquarters because they knew she had a mean left hook and a temper.

Quinn's group of interns stood together near the front. Well, everyone except for her. She could have tried to join them, but she had learned over the past few days that Elena ran things, and that she didn't like having Quinn around. At lunches, there was almost never a sixth chair at their table, and the one time there was, so many purses and coats were piled on it that the message was very clear: You're not welcome.

"Not a fan of the Russian princess, eh?" Riya said as they wove their way through the crowd.

"We don't really see eye to eye," Quinn said.

"Well, how could you? Her heels are like six inches tall," Riya said, standing on the tip toes of her sneakers to emphasize.

Riya was fun and an excellent teacher. In the past week, Quinn had spent every night in the gym with her, followed by a shower in the training center, and then two hours of extra research at her terminal. It had only taken a day or two to realize that if she didn't go to bed until nearly midnight, she wouldn't have to deal with her less than pleasant peers.

Up front, PR staff positioned photographers and made sure everyone in the front row was smiling and picture perfect. The ceremony would begin any minute.

Quinn looked up from her watch, and then let her eyes drift back to her team. Her generalization that all of them were horrible might have been a little unfair. Sure, there were some bad eggs. But Luan had barely said two words to her, so she couldn't really judge him without any information, and Finn—he was a different matter entirely.

A tall woman with her blonde hair in a low bun and lips painted with bright red lipstick stepped up on the podium. Her navy suit looked expensive and pinned to her lapel was a golden brooch. Her smile was perfectly practiced as she waved to the cameras.

"Wow, what a punch in the gut," Riya said, shaking her head.

She was right.

They were making Ambassador Keegan introduce Richard Camden. Nothing could be more humiliating for the Ambassador. She'd run against him during the election with a platform that was strongly opposed to the GPP. In fact, Keegan had a drastically different solution for the world's power issues. Quinn knew quite a few people, her mother included, that had supported Keegan before she started pushing for nuclear power, but after she made her infrastructure plans clear to the public, Camden was a shoe-in for the presidency.

"Thank you all for coming out today," Keegan started, her grin looking forced. "Richard Camden's leadership on the GPP has catapulted our government into a new age. Every corner of the globe now has access to affordable and sustainable energy. From the iciest mountain tops to the most remote deserts—all citizens can power everything they need for the most minimal of costs. Because of his and Vice President Gamble's efforts, we are all connected, all together. Please join me in welcoming President Camden to the stage."

Keegan stepped down from the stage as the crowd erupted in applause. Camden's hair always looked the same. His tie was never out of place. He was the perfect politician. Quinn clapped with everyone else but watched Keegan sadly.

Why would they make her introduce him? It was like they were forcing her to publicly admit to being wrong for the protests she'd made at the beginning of the GPP.

"Maybe she volunteered to introduce him," Quinn speculated aloud.

"Nah, I'm sure they twisted her arm. I bet she didn't have a choice," Riya said.

As Camden riled up the crowd into a patriotic frenzy, Keegan made a beeline for the exit, but Director Lehi intercepted her and whispered in her ear. The empty smile melted from the Ambassador's face, and a second later she disappeared out of the courtyard.

Quinn narrowed her eyes. What the hell was that all about?

She turned attention back to the stage, noting that Camden's daughter, Alexandria, was missing from her usual spot on his left. That was strange, but now that Quinn thought about it, she hadn't seen Alexandria on stage in a while.

Once the ribbon was cut, the crowd started to thin. Quinn dropped by the vending machines to grab a quick bite and then dragged herself across the UNID complex to enjoy another thrilling day of dodging six-inch heels.

Some days were slow in the intelligence world, so when the intern team didn't have a case to work on, they were told to use the time for "research." For Quinn, that meant digging through news reports and old case files to get better at the strengths of her peers. But, for everyone else, research meant talking. A lot.

"There's no place more beautiful than Lake Baikal in the winter, Oliver. The water is so pure that the ice is like glass."

"Transparent ice? Now there's something you don't see every day," Finlay said, shaking his to-go cup for emphasis. "Geddit?" he said to Quinn.

She smiled. She didn't join in on their conversation, but she also didn't completely block out their chatter with her earbuds.

"You're not going to impress me with a lake, dear," Oliver piped up. "Australia's got beautiful coastlines, exotic wildlife, and, best of all, it's not freezing."

"Of course, the exotic wildlife all wants to eat you," Finn quipped.

"You ain't lying." Oliver lifted the hem of his shirt.

Quinn was just wondering why he thought Australia's fauna and animal population had been a good segue to showing off his abs, when he pointed out a scar on his right side.

"I was hiking about a year ago, and a cobra got me good. I was two hours into the woods when it happened. It took everything I had to get out of the forest and to a doctor. A lesser man would have died."

Gretchen's gasp made Quinn roll her eyes. She couldn't resist the snort that came out of her.

"What's so funny, Lehi?" Oliver said, lowering his shirt and glaring.

Quinn smiled at her terminal and pulled up a different news stream. "Cobras aren't indigenous to Australia, and that's an appendectomy scar."

A tense silence followed until Finlay burst into giggles. "She got you, mate."

IT WAS A TUESDAY EVENING when the lights first flickered off. She'd been working well into the night at her terminal. Her eyes were watering from the intensity of her focus, and she had plans to stay until the janitorial staff shooed her out of the office to clean.

Her desk had powered down suddenly, leaving her in complete darkness. Her eyes had searched the room for any sliver of light, but the basement of UNID was shrouded in shadow. She had groaned loudly and then used the light from her data-pad to find her way up the staircase and across the grounds back to the dormitory.

By the next morning, the power had come back on. The night before, the blackout had seemed a mere insignificant inconvenience, but at daybreak the chain of command was alive with activity. One superior passed it down to another until it landed on Agent Hart's desk.

Higher-ups were concerned about the brief outage the night before, and they wanted the lowly interns to conduct an investigation.

There had been some resistance from her compatriots about whether something as minor as an outage was worth their time, but the more Quinn dug into it, the more concerned she became.

A facility like UNID was never meant to be without power. They were set up as a top priority for the power grid, only trumped by certain facilities in the capital. UNID held all the secrets, and a power failure, even a short one, could mean their network was vulnerable. It could be just the opportunity hackers needed to infiltrate their defenses.

So, this was concerning enough to raise the alarms at Headquarters, but more alarming was that it wasn't just UNID that had powered down; it was everyone. The entire country, *the entire world*—everyone had lost power for a few hours. Everyone.

It was easy to ignore in D.C., where citizens had been tucked away in their beds and ignorant to the world, but on the other side of the planet—in Petrova's homeland, for instance—the powerless hours had passed in the daylight.

The new electrical towers were designed to be self-sustaining—flawless. They would only need the smallest bit of upkeep and would supply the world with clean energy for hundreds of years. President Camden's entire political platform had been based on the idea, and he had won by a landslide.

This hiccup could be nothing, but what if it were something bigger? What if the grid wasn't delivering on what had been promised?

Hart had opened the orders as soon as they hit his desk. He'd taken a moment to pull out his reading glasses, which looked oddly out of place on him. He cleared his throat and then explained what was being asked of them. "Cadets, the first objective of your mission is to find out if our systems were breached, and if they were, we need to know what information was accessed and by who."

Quinn smirked. She glanced at her nemesis and from the tight pursing of the Russian's lips, she figured Elena had caught on to how instrumental Quinn's expertise would be in this assignment.

Quinn flexed her fingers. Sure, she wasn't the go-to girl for ballistics or forensic accounting, but this mission played to her strengths and was just what she needed to outshine the competition.

"There is a second objective," Hart continued, "but the director herself wants to address the matter at the end of the day. For now, figure out what you can about a possible breach. The rest is classified."

Quinn hated secrets.

PEOPLE LIKED DEFINITIVE answers. They liked to know that the sun would *always* come up, that their favorite teams would *never* lose, and that every spec of information had been examined, categorized, and filed away.

Unfortunately, most mysteries in this world could rarely be solved to that level of certainty. Sometimes, you had to do your best to find the answers, and then accept that part of the unknown would always remain in the dark.

There were no red flags that signaled someone had infiltrated UNID's system. The access records were clean. Activity died out when the power went off, and then started up as soon as the grid was live again.

She checked every known way that outside users could get into a network, then every path she would have taken if she didn't have her own UNID username and password.

She wasn't one hundred percent positive, but she'd done all that she could in the few short hours since Hart had given them the assignment.

And what had everyone else done while she did what she did best?

Well, as it turned out, Luan wasn't completely useless at prowling around a network. His background was in data analysis, and he'd quickly caught on to her search methods and followed suit.

Finn had sat at his station, swiping through the new reports coming in from all over the world. Finlay was well suited to monitor the news feeds. He knew almost every major language on the planet and could stumble his way through the others. Other teams at UNID were having to wait for translations to be posted, but they had Finn.

Elena had sat with her spine ramrod straight in a chair beside Quinn's desk. She'd frowned, complained, and tapped her foot impatiently for hours.

And Oliver and Gretchen? They were nowhere to be found, but Quinn had her theories. It looked like it was Gretchen's turn to follow Oliver into an abandoned office. Quinn wondered if Elena had drawn the same conclusion, and if she were heartbroken. It was unlikely—she'd have to have a heart for it to be broken.

Quinn didn't care that not everyone was pulling their weight. She'd done her best to complete their first objective, and if she knew her mother, they weren't the only group on this assignment. Some other highly qualified personnel were working the same mission that they were.

"There's nothing," Quinn said and then winced. Right. She should avoid definitive answers like that. "Nothing that I can see, at least." She didn't know why she was saying all of this to Elena. She definitely wasn't her boss, even though she had been breathing down her neck for hours.

"Luan?" Elena started, "Did you find anything?"

He shook his head.

"No news is good news, right? We don't want to find anything," Finn said.

"It's great news," a voice said behind them.

Quinn spun around in her desk chair, trying not to seem too eager. Her mother stayed by the door, looking annoyed as her eyes swept over the empty chairs in the room.

They had been waiting all day for the second objective, and all four seemed to hold their breath.

Director Lehi didn't make them wait, and she didn't sugarcoat the request. "Going forward, this will be your top priority. We will not be delegating any further assignments to the team until this matter is settled. I don't think the power outage was an accident. I think our government is under attack. I want you to tell me who is responsible for this failure and how they did it so I can stop them."

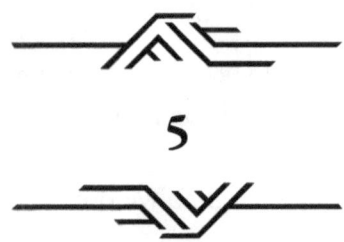

5

A WEEK LATER THE INVESTIGATION hadn't moved forward an inch. Everyone was getting antsy, and Quinn's team was starting to lose focus. She was on her way upstairs after a few grueling hours in the lab when the door to a janitorial closet whipped open.

Gretchen's hair looked uncharacteristically fluffy, and her lipstick wasn't quiet in place on her lips. Fearing she'd get caught spying, Quinn dropped behind a stack of storage crates that always seemed to be abandoned in the UNID basement. She felt ridiculous hiding but was enjoying her newfound role of cheesy on-screen detective.

Gretchen disappeared around the corner that led to the elevators and, a moment later, Oliver emerged from the same doorway. He had a pleased look on his face and Gretchen's garish lipstick on his white collar.

He was definitely hooking up with both Elena and Gretchen. Case closed.

Gross.

She wished she had made more progress on the real assignment, but hey, at least she'd solved one mystery. Really it made her feel more icky than accomplished. Quinn hustled her way up the stairs and out of the building.

"Hey, Q! Wait up!" Finn shouted.

Quinn's heart took a little leap as she waited under one of the solar lights that lit the walkway. The little nickname he'd given her that first day made her silly giggle on the inside while on the outside she tried her best to remain cool. Aloof. Was he buying it? His grin made her think not.

"Let me guess?" she joked. "You're still sore over that left hook I snuck in under your guard yesterday?"

His eyes turned hard for a moment, which was out of character for him. Then his cheeks flushed pink in embarrassment, making her feel guilty for the comment. The flash of anger was gone as quickly as it began, and his customary charming grin was back. Guys could be so much more sensitive about things than she ever expected.

"Hey, anytime you want to lay me out—I'm in, but I could think of more pleasant ways to accomplish it."

Quinn snorted. Snorted!

Her face flooded with embarrassment, and she looked away as they shuffled up the path. Was he flirting with her? That comment was fairly pointed, much more so than his usual casual charm.

"Uh—sorry, what was it you wanted to do to me—I mean say to me?" Gah! What was wrong with her!

"Actually, I was thinking about how tomorrow's our day off."

"Yes! Finally, right? But, I'll probably still spend most of it training. How about you?"

"I was thinking about spending some of it with my favorite intern."

"Oh yeah? You and Luan gonna get in some quality bro time?"

"Ha. You're a riot, Q," he said, as they strolled side by side along the moonlit pathway to the dorms. "He still hasn't spoken a word to me. Unless you count grunts. Which I don't."

"Don't worry, you aren't alone. He usually just points to the data on the screen that he wants me to read."

"Yeah, but he's talked to you! I heard him ask you about regression analysis for data modeling during that last assignment. He pretends I don't exist."

"I think he talks to me because we have a similar skill set."

"Meh. Anyway, I didn't want to talk about Pillay. I wanted to ask you out."

"Out?" she asked, stunned. "Like, on a date?"

"Yeah, out—"

"But we're competing against each other. I'm the enemy."

"What? No! We're a team, Quinn."

"Are you kidding me? You can't be that naïve. We all want the same spot."

"It's not that way for me."

Quinn stopped walking. She needed to see his face while he spouted this nonsense.

"Okay, I can see you don't exactly believe me," he said, sliding his hands into his front pockets.

"I think you are full of crap, yes."

"Look, this is how it is. Would I like to get the slot and say I'd been the best? Yes. But I don't need the job. I'm not even sure I'd take it if I got to the top."

Her mouth fell open. "Why on earth would you be putting yourself through this program if you didn't even want it?"

"I have another job waiting for me."

"Another job?" This stunned her more than anything. There was no other job. Not for her. UNID was it for her. If she didn't get it—she didn't even know what her life would entail. Just a black hole of meaninglessness. Anger began to well up.

How dare he compete against her and jeopardize her dreams when he didn't really want it!

She wasn't sure what happened next. It was a bit of a blur. At first, she felt a little dizzy, then her fingers began to tingle. The next thing she knew, Finn was on his back, and her knuckles were stinging.

"Oh my—Finn! I'm so sorry! I don't know what just came over me." She dropped to her knees beside him. He was already sitting up, rubbing his jaw. It was dark, but the path was lit well enough to see a red spot welling under his chin.

"What the hell, Quinn?"

"I can't—I mean, I don't—"

"Do you mind telling me what that was for?" he asked angrily.

Why had she just laid into him like that?

"When you said you had another job, that you probably wouldn't even take it if you got it... I don't know—you could have slapped me and had the same effect. It's like, the thing I value most in the world right now is just meh to you, and I could lose to someone who doesn't even care?" She shook her head, dumbfounded.

"Look, UNID is an amazing opportunity. That goes without saying. When I applied here I thought it was a long shot, and my parents were keen for me to try. I also applied to my dream job at the University International to study and teach under International's lead language and diplomacy expert. I found out I was accepted to both just days apart. I know what I want and UNID would be great, don't get me wrong, but at International I'd get to spend all day every day in language. If I get in here, I have to work on other skills. Like you have."

Quinn flushed at the praise, but he continued.

"My parents want this job more than I do. To them, it's the better prize, but for me, the other way is easier and probably going to make me happier in the long run."

Finn had scooted off the path to lean back against the building, so Quinn moved to sit next to him. She didn't say anything for a while, just tried to sort through her feelings about his decisions. She understood wanting to please his parents. She wished UNID was what her mom wanted for her. It would make life so much more pleasant. But, if she were being honest, Finn was probably not her biggest competition here. He was adorable and made her heart speed up when he was near, but he wasn't producing in a way that made her feel threatened. Mostly he followed her lead.

"Sorry again for hitting you. I guess it's just difficult to imagine someone not wanting the thing I want. I mean, it's amazing here, right? Well, other than being completely ostracized by my coworkers," she said grimly.

"Don't worry about it. I understand. However, you could make up for the bruising you just gave my masculine ego and go out with me tomorrow."

Oh yeah, that!

"What did you have in mind?" she asked. It seemed a little crazy that he'd still want to go on a date with her, but hey, who was she to complain?

"I've always wanted to go on the Sky Wheel, but I've never been. I think tomorrow is going to be another clear night like tonight, so we should be able to see everything for miles."

She'd been on the Sky Wheel once when it was first completed. It was pretty touristy, as most of D.C. was, so it was something the locals tended to avoid. But she could see the appeal. The giant Ferris wheel had been built a decade ago with the intent to show up the London Eye.

"Sure, if you are willing to risk your face in my presence then, yeah, I'll go."

"Great," he said, standing once more. He reached for her hand to help her up and for a second, they just stood there like that. Staring.

Maybe he would kiss her.

She'd been kissed by exactly three guys. One was a long-term boyfriend that just didn't make it through the separation of college and the others were insignificant. It had been a while though, and she suddenly worried about things like whether she'd eaten onions at dinner, whether she was too short or too tall.

The moment stretched—his hand still holding hers.

"Attention," the loudspeaker boomed. "All cadets are reminded to attend the morning sprints on the lawn at 0600 hours." The announcement trilled out over the campus, and the moment was broken.

She couldn't decide if she were relieved or not as he turned and they walked back to the dorm. They separated at the bottom of the stairs to make their ways back to their rooms, and as Quinn fell asleep that night she played the walk back over and over in her head. He'd held her hand the whole way.

THE NEXT DAY BROKE bright and beautiful. She rushed through the mandatory sprints—on their "day off" giving it a little more effort than usual to finish fast. The running was already much easier than when she'd first started. Though she still wasn't doing great on distance runs. Today she couldn't wait to get to her training session with Riya to tell her all the juicy details from last night. At the very least, Riya would get a kick out of the punch retelling.

Riya was in the ring when she walked into the training center later that morning. Quinn stood back to watch. She'd never seen her square off against anyone—she was always just killing the punching bag.

Her opponent was a really hot—and quite shirtless—younger guy. Probably early twenties. His skin tone was slightly darker than Riya's, but his hair was equally black, except cut short with just a little curl to it. She'd guess he was Hispanic. He had a full six pack of rock hard abs, which Riya's slight nineteen-year-old fists were currently pummeling.

She flinched as she watched her friend deliver a kick to those gorgeous abs, which caused an audible air sucking sound to escape her opponent. Then before she could move out of reach, the guy gave her a nasty punch to the ribs. Watching them, Quinn felt like they were pretty evenly matched, but Riya worked her short stature to her advantage, and she was quick to jab or kick and make a fast retreat, wearing him down slowly. She heard his name, Miguel, called out by a few of the bystanders as they cheered the two agents on.

Then, in a masterful move, Riya managed to climb up his side, get a leg around his neck, and use all her momentum to pull him down under her, squeezing off his air until he tapped out. The whole thing happened so fast her head was spinning.

After a moment of recovery, Miguel stood up, and then he and Riya bumped fists. He said something to her, close enough and low enough that Quinn doubted anyone but Riya could hear it. Riya shook her head in reply, a slight grin on her face, but Miguel's expression turned stony before he stepped off through the ropes and grabbed a bottle of water from a friend nearby.

Riya turned to exit in the opposite direction, until she saw Quinn waiting on the edge of the small crowd.

"Hey! Did you catch the fight?"

"I did indeed," she said, moving away from the wall where she'd been leaning. "I'm glad we're friends, and I'm not on the receiving end of those kicks."

"Girl, you are holding your own these days. You'll get there."

"Ha! I don't think my few weeks of training are going to rival your years of fighting any time soon. However, I have a confession to make that I'm embarrassed about, but I know you'll probably enjoy."

Riya looked intrigued as she dropped into a chair to the side of the ring, and Quinn began to wrap her hands for their session.

"Well," Riya said, breath still coming in hard, "I'm all ears, now you've dangled that bit of salacious carrot."

"Last night, Finn—I've told you about Finn, right?"

Riya nodded. "Sure, cute guy, languages, wants to get in your pants."

"He doesn't—"

She paused as Riya's eyebrow notched up in challenge.

"I mean okay, maybe. Because last night, he asked me out on a date."

"That's good, right? I mean, I'm assuming you like this guy since you turn kind of goofy and smiley whenever you mention him."

"Well, yeah, I think I do, but then I punched him."

Riya's bark of laughter filled the large open space, causing several people to turn and look for the source. Riya ignored the attention and held up a fist for Quinn to bump. "Right on. I don't understand it, but yeah. You've turned into a regular brawler. What was wrong? Did he get all condescending and sexist on you?"

"Well no, I didn't punch him because of the date. You won't believe what he told me!" Quinn said, throwing up her hands. "He doesn't even care if he gets this job. He's got another one he wants more waiting in the wings. This is just like, some kind of strange effort to make his parents happy."

Riya's face was skeptical. "Why would anyone put themselves through this circus if they didn't want it?"

"Beats me. Here I am *straining* my relationship with mom because I want it so bad, and he doesn't even care if he wins. Which was why I punched him. My frustration with this whole process just shot through my fist and into his jaw. I swear I might come unhinged if he actually does beat me."

Riya shook her head. "Okay, enough chitchat. Let's start with punch kick combos."

"Yes, coach." Quinn followed Riya's direction and threw a left jab, left jab, kick into the bag.

Riya continued. "So, no date, huh?"

"Oh, no. We're going out tonight."

"Wait," Riya said, halting her mid-swing. "You punched him in the face, and he still wanted to take you out?"

"Yeah, crazy, huh?"

"The boy must have it bad."

Quinn grinned, thinking about what might come of the evening. Then she remembered something she'd wanted to ask Riya earlier. "Hey, that guy you were fighting—Miguel. What was he saying to you after the fight? I mean, if you don't mind telling me," she clarified, suddenly realizing what a personal question she might have just asked.

"Well, Miss Nosy," her friend replied, "Miguel and I may have celebrated my selection a couple months ago with a lot of alcohol and a hasty one-night stand he wants to repeat. But I'm not just an intern anymore, and we were assigned to the same team. Even if I was interested in having a boyfriend, which I'm not, it wouldn't be someone I have to work with. That's just asking for trouble."

"Makes sense. I doubt this thing with Finn goes anywhere, but at least I know only one of us will work here when it's over...or neither."

"Hey, don't talk like that." Riya pointed to the bag for Quinn to pick back up. "You need to get this job, so I've got a good desker in my ear when I'm out there. The current guy is super slow delivering my forensics results."

Quinn laughed and got back to her combos. She'd come a long way. Fighting wasn't bothering her so much anymore. In fact, she was picturing Elena's pretty face with each jab.

QUINN SPENT A FULL hour and a half getting ready for her date with Finn that night. She had rushed back to her mom's house after her training session to find some more casual after-work attire in her monstrous closet. Behind all the outdated tech still cluttering the space from her recent hardware upgrades, she found a cute purple dress that cinched at the waist before flaring outward at her hips. She tossed it in a garment bag and disappeared from the house before her mom could catch her there.

While it was rare for her to go out, it was even more rare for her to be nervous about it. She'd grown up with Karyn Lehi as a role model, and for as long as she could remember, her mother had treated personal relationships as trivial nuisances. Every time Quinn had swooned over a boy at school or gone to see a movie with someone, her mother had scoffed about the time waste.

She made it back to the complex and had barricaded herself in the dorm, scattered makeup all over her desk, and then got to work getting dolled up.

There was a moment while applying eyeliner when she'd paused. Why did Finn like her? Or maybe he didn't. Maybe he was just looking for a way to pass the time, and since it seemed like Oliver had claimed the other two girls with his janitorial closet fumbling, maybe Quinn was the only one left.

She'd shaken that feeling away by the time he'd come to pick her up. It didn't mean anything; she just had some pre-date jitters. She'd beamed her brightest smile at him when she opened her door, and together they had made their way to the Boardwalk, a stretch of carnival booths and small rides that surrounded the Sky Wheel.

At the office, Finn never really looked completely put together. His ties were always hanging loosely and his dress shirts always pushed up to his elbows. But she'd never seen him this casual. He was dressed down in jeans and a dark green T-shirt, looking perfect except for the light bruise on his chin where she had clocked him.

As she had expected, the Boardwalk was flooded with tourists. They were milling between game booths and buying funnel cakes from kitschy stands. She'd always lived in D.C., so this had long been a place to avoid, but Finn seemed to like it.

"Now, *this* is the D.C. I pictured, Q."

"I'm sure it was in the tour guide."

People were rushing past them, and she was feeling overwhelmed at the magnitude of tourists. Then Finn turned toward her and extended his hand, and for a moment, everything seemed picture perfect. At the center was Finlay Evans, the most charming boy she'd ever met, who had made her swoon from the moment he'd glanced in her direction. Framing him were multicolored lights that twinkled and bright game booths with mediocre prizes not meant to be won.

His gorgeous smile nearly knocked her off her feet. Everything about the night felt dream-like and perfect.

"C'mon, Q. Let me win you the biggest stuffed animal in this place." His voice was dripping with charisma, and Quinn felt so lucky to have met him—to be the center of his attention for even one date.

They spent the night going from booth to booth, making their way to the end of the pier that overlooked the Potomac River. They took turns trying to win prizes, but they mostly ended up with cheap loot that wasn't worth keeping. There was one very small stuffed bear that was kind of cute.

When Finn had gifted it to her, she laughed loudly. "I guess this is the biggest stuffed animal they had, huh?"

"I nearly threw my arm out at Skee-Ball, and this is what I get," he said, eyes gleaming with mischief.

At the end of the pier was the enormous Sky Wheel, the biggest in the world. Its carts were large, candy-colored pods. Their glittery paint gleamed from the lights that twinkled around the Boardwalk. They waited in the long line, behind tourists who took pictures every other second. They seemed to be from all over the world because for the past few hours she had heard far more foreign tongues than she had heard English.

Finn was leaning against the metal rails that ran the length of the line. He snorted quietly.

"What?" she said, eyeing him as they moved forward.

"People will say anything when they think no one knows their language."

Quinn grinned. "Like what? Tell me!" she demanded quietly.

She sucked in a breath when he slid a hand down to the small of her back.

His voice dropped to a whisper. "Well, this lovely German couple is in the heat of a rather personal argument."

Quinn glanced at them. They were all smiles, but now that Finn had said something, they did seem rather tense, and the woman had huffed once or twice.

"What are they fighting about?"

"His mother."

Quinn laughed. They walked forward to the massive wheel, and she looked up at the empty carts to see what color they would get.

"The women behind us are speaking Portuguese, but from their dialect, they are definitely from Brazil."

"And what are they saying?" She brushed her hair behind her ear and subtly glanced at the four women.

"Well, their friend is in the restroom, and ever since she stepped away, they have been tearing into her. Rude, really, but still very entertaining."

She noticed when their friend joined them back in line, they were all very friendly with one another.

Finn's talents were very powerful for a UNID agent. She knew a few languages, but he was a living Rosetta Stone.

"Ladies first," Finn said as they were ushered into the large teal blue cart. Inside was a row of seats and binocular stands that could be used to look across the Boardwalk and out on the city.

They began their ascent, and Quinn smiled when the breeze blew through. Their rise was slowed by other passengers boarding below. She could hear the German couple in the cart above, and now that they were alone, their argument no longer held the tense politeness it had before.

The city expanded as they rose above the horizon. She turned to Finn. He was watching her, a speculative look behind his dark brown eyes, but when he met her gaze, his charming smile slid back into place.

She could feel the shift in the air as he slid closer to her in the cart. The intensity of his gaze made her nervous, and she decided breaking the silence would ease some tension.

"Say we get to the end of the program, and I get the job. Then you take the job you want at University International," Quinn said. "Do we ever see each other again?"

He smirked. "I certainly hope so."

Her heart leapt in her chest. Maybe Finn wasn't playing Oliver's game. Maybe he wasn't just after a quick fling with a peer.

"Speaking of the job," Finn started, "have you made any headway into our assignment?"

A Ferris wheel was hardly the place to talk about their top-secret mission. The ride lurched as the final passengers boarded. It was unlikely they would be heard, but she still wouldn't go into the specifics out in public.

"The Director's concerns appear to be founded. I have some hunches I'm following, but there's nothing solid yet," Quinn said vaguely.

Finn's eyebrows shot up. "Very cryptic," he said, looking a little put out. "We're on the same team, remember? You can trust me."

Quinn laughed. "I know that, silly. We can go over my files when we're back in a secure area. For now, let's just enjoy the night, okay?"

The wheel brought them to the top and then started bringing their cart back down.

"Of course," Finn said, sliding his hand into hers and lacing their fingers together.

The city was beautiful, and all the lights were rushing by as the ride continued. She was awestruck as she approached the windows.

Then, something very curious happened. In the distance, she could see a darkness rushing across the city like a shockwave. It tore through the carnival, and the strings of bulbs flickered off one after the other. The ride lurched hard, their cart swinging forcefully as the Boardwalk powered down. She grabbed at a safety handle, and they scrambled to get back to the seats.

"Another blackout," Finn said aloud.

The tourists above and below them complained loudly in different tongues. In English, a handheld megaphone announced below that they would work on getting everyone out. When the complaints weren't quelled, Finn started to repeat the announcement loudly in all the languages he had heard around them, and slowly the crowd quieted down.

Quinn looked toward the capital building and toward UNID and felt fear seep into her. The country was under attack, and she was stranded at the top of a Ferris wheel. Sometimes the blackouts lasted hours. She couldn't help anyone from here.

Quick short breaths tore from her lungs.

Finn's hands were warm on her face in the next moment. "Everything is okay, Q. They are going to get us down. I need you to stay calm," he said in a deep soothing tone.

She nodded and tried very hard to get herself under control.

"That's it," he said, fingertips rubbing little circles at the base of her scalp. "We're going to be fine."

Her breathing steadied, and she got lost in his eyes, lost in the deep richness of his voice.

In the moonlight, she could barely see his smile, but it was sweet and inviting. He leaned forward, his lips brushing against hers, and then every worry slipped away. The power would come back on soon, and until then, she had Finn; she had this moment—this night.

They kissed while the Boardwalk employees rotated the wheel, slowly rescuing the passengers. When the Portuguese women disembarked, Quinn and Finn pulled away from each other and tried to look as normal as possible when the outside door was unlatched, and they were escorted off the ride.

Her feet barely touched the ground when the lights flooded back on, almost blinding in contrast to the inky darkness of the last several minutes. Relieved murmuring buzzed around them.

"Let's get back to HQ," she said, pulling him toward the parking deck. "You know everyone will be there working this latest glitch."

They shared giddy smiles and held hands all the way to the car. She couldn't believe her luck. This charming man liked her, and she was without a doubt breaking every one of her mother's mantras because Quinn definitely liked him back. Maybe she wouldn't have to choose between having her dream job and getting the guy. Maybe she could have both.

6

WHEN THE POWER HAD gone out on her date with Finn, it had felt like an amazingly special romantic moment—his voice centering her, his lips moving in closer. It was perfect. But, once they returned, there was nothing even remotely romantic about the situation at UNID.

Controlled chaos was a more accurate description.

The building reminded Quinn of a beehive with everyone bustling about to execute whatever job they'd been assigned by the queen—and there was no doubt who the queen was. Her data-pad was filled with her mother's public statements of complete dedication to investigating the blackouts and UNID-only directives to all agents detailing her expectations.

As she and Finn quickly made their way to the intern lab, she could make out faint voices hurriedly saying things like "the Director wants this right away" and "the Director needs..." It was obvious her mother was taking this very seriously. So Quinn put on her best "Director Lehi" impersonation as they walked through the lab doors, determined to take control of this situation.

But before she could utter the first word of her prepared speech, Hart called out a reprimand.

"Glad you could finally grace us with your presence. Luckily you're just in time. We're about to be briefed on our new assignment."

"New assignment? Is it not the blackout?" she asked, confused.

Quinn looked to Finn, but he simply shrugged. The other interns appeared impatient.

"Why don't we find out?" he said, pulling up a file and displaying it on the large screen. It was a video briefing recorded just an hour ago. It must have been sent right before the blackout.

"Reporting from Fairfax, this is Senior Agent Wilton. Local police were called late yesterday evening when Dr. Henry Laycomb, Chief Engineer of the GPP, was reported missing. Five hours later a second scientist, Peter Albright, was reported missing. Both men were central to the configuration of the GPP. Once the connection was made, they notified us. It's been three hours on the case now, and we have not been able to locate the men. My team has a bad feeling about this one. So, as the Senior Field Agent, I am recommending an increased priority on this case. All field case logs have been uploaded to UNID servers."

The clip cut out, and the room was silent for one tense moment. Then, all hell broke loose.

Quinn rushed to her station and slid into her chair so quickly it began to roll off to the side. She caught the lip of her desk and reeled herself back in. Every intern began to pull up the field notes. They weren't the only ones on this case. From what she could see, every intel spec team at UNID HQ was feeding leads into the case logs.

It couldn't be a coincidence that two prominent scientists on the GPP would go missing at the same time they were experiencing intermittent blackouts.

Quinn was running through phone records of the missing men while Finn sat beside her reading interview transcripts. Dr. Laycomb had been working as a professor at George Washington ever since the completion of the GPP. His mobile texts and calls as well as his work correspondence had already been scoured, and nothing out of the ordinary was found. But she had a hunch. From experience, she'd seen that professors rarely received calls directly to their offices. They were often routed to the department admin to save them the hassle of dealing with disgruntled students.

Quinn pulled up records for the whole department. The desk of the science department's admin line had received a call just a half hour before he was last seen. That call came from a number where the first three digits perfectly matched UNID's trunk line. It was an extremely curious coincidence. Why would someone from UNID be calling him? Just minutes before he went missing? From what she'd seen of the case log entries, no one had mentioned contacting him prior to his disappearance. The ID on the university's end wouldn't tell her anything, because UNID numbers were restricted. So she pulled up the directory to see where the number led inside the complex. But, before she could enter the number, they were suddenly cast into complete darkness.

The whole room went quiet.

The gentle hum of machines she'd never noticed in the background were now eerily silent. In the deep recesses of their basement lab, she couldn't see her own hand in front of her face.

She felt around blindly for something to turn on, then remembered her data-pad. The screen lit up and everyone else in the room followed suit. Each intern's face glowed from the small light, and every face looked a little lost.

Agent Hart tapped on his screen. "The servers are off-line. Networks are down. Everyone just settle down for the moment. Power should come back up soon, and then we'll get back to work."

Oliver cracked his neck. Elena tapped her heels impatiently. Quinn counted. She'd counted out five minutes when the tension became too much.

"What if it doesn't come back tonight? These guys are still missing," she said.

Gretchen scoffed. "The power can't stay off forever. There are dozens of fail-safes built into the grid. We'll be back online soon."

But they weren't. Minutes turned into an hour. Oliver finally stood and yawned. "It's late. I'm going to bed. Call me when the power comes back on. We're useless until it does."

Part of her couldn't help but agree. She'd depended on technology for answers her whole life. What could they do without it? Then she thought about these scientists. Their families were out there. Worried. Every minute they remained missing decreased the likelihood they would be found. Then an idea popped into her head. She needed to find Riya.

Grasping Finn's hand, she gently squeezed, silently asking him to go along with her plan. "That sounds like a good idea, Oliver. We don't know how long this will take, but we won't be any good to anyone if we haven't had any rest."

"Alright then," Finn chimed, "we'll just go now."

They both headed to the door behind Oliver. Quinn crossed her fingers Hart would agree. She wished she could bring the whole team along on her plan, but they would never follow her lead. Finn could be trusted to help instead of getting in the way.

Hart yawned. "It's not a bad plan. When the power comes back, I expect your butts back in these chairs in fifteen minutes."

Echoes of agreement filtered through their shuffling sounds, as they tried to avoid knocking into something hidden in the darkness.

Once out the doors, they carefully climbed the stairs to the main floor. Quinn really wanted to talk to her mother about her plan, but considering she was on one of the top floors, she really didn't want to waste her energy like that, and she was still dressed for her date and in desperate need of her tennis shoes before she attempted a sixteen-story climb. Riya's squadron was just two flights up—much more doable.

The lobby was even more chaotic than when they'd arrived. People were trying to move just as quickly, but the glow of data-pads was insufficient to prevent pile-ups. Quinn barely dodged an elbow to the face as someone barreled into the person next to her. Finn pulled on her hand just in time to avoid the collision. The stairs going up were even trickier. Masses of people were pouring down with the elevators out of commission, and they were having to fight against the tide. She made a beeline to Riya's work station only to find it empty. Miguel strode past quickly, and she grabbed his arm just before he moved out of reach.

"Where's Riya?"

"I don't know. She was sent to the forensics lab to review some of the evidence on the missing persons case just before the power blew."

"Hey," Finn said, grabbing her elbow. "What are you up to?"

"Are we done?" Miguel asked impatiently.

"Yeah, I'll find her," she replied.

Miguel strode away in a hurry.

Quinn turned back toward the stairs, but Finn pulled her to a stop.

"Do you mind clueing me in on this, or are you going to just haul me from room to room and leave me to guess?"

She sighed.

"I want to go look at the last place Dr. Laycomb was seen—his office at the university. Investigators spoke to several of his colleagues, but the department admin wasn't on their list." Quinn didn't know why she didn't tell him about the call from UNID, but something was nagging at her to keep it to herself for now. She didn't like sharing her ideas before she'd had time to fully develop them. It was probably weird of her. Okay, maybe egotistical was the right word, but she wanted everything she said out loud to be right, one hundred percent of the time. And the call could have been nothing, probably had to do with the investigation they were all contributing to on the small blackouts. But she wanted to know who made the call. They might know something.

"Quinn, we don't go into the field. We're intel agents. Actually, we aren't even that; we're just interns."

"I know. That's why we need Riya. She knows the field, and right now, we can't be her eye-in-the-sky. We need to go together. She hasn't combed through the data like we have, so we will be able to see any patterns while she conducts the investigation."

Finn ran a hand though his already tousled locks, looking more serious than he ever had. "It's not that I think it's a bad idea, but two people are missing, and you want to go expose yourself to a dangerous situation? We'll be walking in blind. No sat imagery. No bots. Just our brains, her brawn, and empty data-pads."

"Yeah, that's about it. But I just have a feeling something is there. Think about it. If we find them, they'd have to give one of us the job. Maybe both of us. Imagine how your parents would react when you and I solve this thing."

His eyes lit up. He tapped his fingers against his leg and seemed to be weighing his choices. "Okay, Q. I'm in. Let's go find Laycomb's admin."

Quinn grabbed his hand once more and pulled him back to the stairs. It was pure luck that as they made their way down to the forensics lab, Riya was just stepping out through the swinging double doors.

"Riya!"

She turned, and her frustrated scowl morphed to a grin. "A little fancy for the office, don't you think?" she asked, indicating Quinn's dolled-up appearance.

"A change is definitely in order before we head out."

"Oh yeah? Where are you going?"

"When I said we, I meant you too."

"Sorry, I'm still cataloging evidence. With paper tags! Gotta love old-school."

"I have a hunch on the missing person case. I need you to come with us."

"What kind of hunch involves a couple of deskers leaving their lab?" she asked, her brow lifted in doubt.

Quinn gave her the same spiel she'd told Finn—leaving out the call, but still mentioning the lack of admin interview in the case logs.

"I'm in, but you realize this is completely against protocol, right? If your hunch is good, it will likely pay off. If it's not, you will probably take a lot of heat. Especially if the power comes back on and you can't get back here quickly. The university is a thirty-minute drive."

She looked to Finn. "Not backing out, are you?"

"No. I'm in," he said, one arm circling her waist.

"Alright," Riya shrugged. "You go change, and I'll grab some tactical cover gear. Meet me outside your dorm in twenty."

THEY PULLED UP TO THE science department building not much later. The drive there had been strange. All the buildings they passed sat in what appeared to be shrouded abandon, while cars lit up the highway. Most vehicles were still running, but a few had run down their charge and sat forgotten on the side of the road. The trip took longer than usual because every intersection had turned into a four-way stop. By the time they arrived, it was the middle of the night, and there was no one around. Everything was quiet and dark. Only a couple street lights, solar relics of the past, were still glowing.

Riya surveyed the building skeptically. "I don't think your missing admin is going to be here to interview."

"She probably wasn't here when they first came by. Maybe we can find a clue to her whereabouts on her desk."

Riya looked unconvinced but turned to climb the stairs anyway, her handgun pointed at the floor, as she and Finn followed close behind. The doors swung open soundlessly, the locking mechanisms down along with the power. The whole situation was strange in its absurdity. Nothing in their world seemed to function without power.

They used the glow of their flashlights to follow the signs to the staff offices. The admin's desk sat in the center of an open space with several doors just off it. Laycomb's name marked the one in the center.

Riya glanced at the desk and then strode toward the door beyond. "I'm going to check out his office. I'm sure it's been thoroughly checked, but it can't hurt to look again."

Finn seemed uninterested in the space entirely as Quinn searched through desk drawers. The woman who worked here—Nathalie Singleton, according to the stationery on the surface—kept an immaculate desk. Rifling through the few contents of Nathalie's space, she found nothing of interest. She wanted to check the phone and find that number again. She had a downloaded copy of the UNID directory on her data-pad, but the phone line here was dead.

"I need to use the loo," Finn said, pulling her out of her thoughts.

"Oh, yeah sure. I think I saw a sign around the corner," she told him.

"Once I'm done, I think we should probably get back. I don't think there's anything here."

He hadn't even looked, but okay.

"Alright, just one more minute. I want to be sure we haven't missed anything."

He shrugged indifferently and turned, disappearing around the dark hallway.

No worries, she'd just had an idea anyway. She unhooked the power cable from Ms. Singleton's phone, then pulled the retractable cable from her data-pad and slid the connector in. The phone lit up, and Quinn barely suppressed a joyful hurrah. Hitting the Recent Calls button, she tapped down to the records from the day before. The first three digits of the number she'd been looking for slid onto the phone's screen, and she quickly copied the rest of the number over to her data-pad. She was about to type it into the directory when Riya stepped out of Laycomb's office. Quinn hurriedly unhooked her pad from the phone.

"Anything?" Riya asked.

"Maybe. I got a number off the phone that I want to look up when we get back. How about you?"

"Not much. This lapel pin was on the floor, wedged between the edge of the carpet and the wall. Have you ever seen it?"

Quinn studied the small "K" surrounded by what looked like an atom. It didn't fit with the spelling of Laycomb's, but maybe it was a science club of some kind. It looked a little familiar.

"I'm not sure. We should be able to know something once the servers come back online, and we can run an object recognition search."

Finn's steps echoed off the hard linoleum as he returned to the room. "Ladies. We ready to get back?"

"Sure," she replied, sliding her data-pad back into her bag.

The three of them piled into the car once more.

"Well, that was a bust," Finn said.

Sure, as far as he knew, that was true. But he sounded so condescending just now. What happened to the sweet guy who'd kissed her on the Sky Wheel? For that, she was keeping her lead to herself. She'd share with Riya once she had a chance to look it up.

They said goodnight once they were back to the dorms. Exhausted, she kind of hoped the power would stay off for at least another six hours so she could get a little rest. From her morning sprints, to her workout, then her date, and the investigation, she was completely worn out.

Finally ready for bed, she tapped on her data-pad once more. Only two percent battery left. She rarely got so low, but she guessed she'd used it more than usual the last several hours, and she hadn't charged it in a couple of days. Before it died, she typed in the number. It took a second to load, running down another percent.

MATCH: DIRECTOR KARYN LEHI

Quinn's heart stopped, just as the screen went blank.

SHE'D HAD THE WORST night of sleep ever, tossing and turning with questions. Then she'd overslept when no alarm sounded at the usual hour. She couldn't remember the last time she'd been awakened by sunlight streaming through her window, but she'd frantically put herself together.

Quinn made her way straight to her mom's office. She pushed away her worry as she climbed the main stairwell. There would be a perfectly good reason for her calling Dr. Laycomb.

Her data-pad was done for. The power was still out. She was taking the stairs in UNID HQ two at a time. She'd asked the man who oversaw the visitor desk in the lobby about her mom's whereabouts. Of course, she would still be in her office, carrying on business as usual.

Her breath was coming in big wheezy lungful by the time she reached the director's floor. She didn't wait to be announced by her mom's assistant but gave one hasty knock before sliding through the door. Her mom was standing at her window looking over the training field below. At Quinn's entrance, she glanced over her shoulder.

"Good news. The backup solar panels I ordered out of storage a couple weeks ago should be installed today. It will only cover the essentials, but we'll be back up and running in no time. I had hoped to share this with the president this morning, but his office just cancelled on me."

"You think of everything," Quinn replied, shutting the door behind her.

"Ha. I wish. Hey, shouldn't you be down there training? I can usually make out your dot at this time of morning."

"You watch my training?" she asked, stunned.

"Just a glance or two when I get a chance. Your times have been improving."

"Yeah," she replied tonelessly, almost forgetting why she was here. "Mom, why were you calling Dr. Laycomb before he disappeared?"

Her mom's grin widened, brightening her face. "Did you figure that out?" she asked, without even a hint of concern. "I was wondering how long it would take for an agent to see it. With the power out, I figured we'd need it back on before anyone could make the connection." She stepped around her desk to lean against the edge. "Obviously, Dr. Laycomb's knowledge of the GPP's infrastructure is invaluable to our current investigation. He's been gathering some ideas on potential areas of vulnerability for me since the first glitch." Her mom's bright face clouded. "Now with him missing, I can't help but wonder if his digging got him into trouble with whomever is responsible. But I'm proud you found the call and followed up. Our best agents didn't get to it before you did."

Quinn's fears melted away. It was as she'd expected. "Mom," she said, moving toward a display case in the corner, trying not to look at her mother's face as she asked the question that had haunted her since before the internship began. "Why don't you want me to get this job? You've discouraged it from the start. I thought you'd be happy for me to follow in your footsteps."

"Oh, Quinn." She sighed deeply. "When I found out you'd submitted an application using your father's name I was pretty livid."

"But, Mom," she cut in, "I just wanted to know I could at least get through the first step on my own merits."

"I understand that, but there are a few reasons I didn't want this for you. Honestly, one of those reasons doesn't show me in the best light," she said, pacing the floor in a rare display of nerves, "but I'll tell you because you should understand."

She paused, seeming to collect her thoughts the same way she would prepare for an official debrief.

"First, you've always been smart. There's no doubt you could run circles around me when it comes to your technical skills. However, an agent has to be more than just brains. Do you remember when you broke that girl's nose in your last karate match?"

Did she have to bring that up?

"You cried every night for a week," her mom said. "Then you never went back. You didn't show the kind of internal grit I've always believed an agent should have."

"But—I've improved. I've made my way up to third in hand-to-hand."

"I know. You've taken everything you were handed and come out better for it. Believe me, I never thought you'd be capable of the brutal way you handled Elena Petrova in your last match."

Quinn laughed at that. "Some people can inspire more rage than others."

She and her mom shared a grin. The first in a long while.

"You said there was more than one reason though."

Her mom pinched at the bridge of her nose. "I hate nepotism. It's like cancer," she said firmly. "Honey, if you get this job, no one would ever trust your accomplishments. My judgement related to you, your team, your assignments, would always be questioned. I refuse to be the director of UNID with you as an agent. I think too much of you, and I want more for myself."

At the vehement tone in her mother's voice, Quinn dropped her head. Respect. That's what it ultimately came down to. Her mother would lose the respect of the organization she loved if Quinn was hired. And Quinn herself would never be able to earn respect, even if she was the best agent the world had ever seen, and she'd never earn respect. That's what her mom was saying.

Looking now at the picture of her mom accepting the director position from President Camden himself, she knew she could never ask her mom to give up everything she'd worked for her whole career. Even through her mother's signature calm expression, she could see her pride as she shook the president's hand.

Wait.

Her attention caught.

In the image, on the lapel of her mother's perfectly pressed suit, there was a pin. It was a K with atoms swirling around it.

A knock at the door had her jumping away.

The door swung open, and her mother's assistant poked her head in.

"Director Lehi. They've just confirmed. Dr. Laycomb's been found. His body was recovered from the Potomac. The agent on the scene is here to report."

"Quinn, we'll finish this discussion later," her mom said, ushering her out as the field agent with the report strode in. The door clicked firmly behind her, leaving Quinn in shock.

7

IF ANYONE AT UNID HAD thought the power outage and disappearances were mere coincidence, there was no denying the correlation now. The lead engineer for the GPP, Henry Laycomb, had been found dead in the Potomac River, and UNID was not only part of the investigation but was central in the effort to keep this new information from the public. The last thing they needed right now was worldwide panic, or at least, more panic than there already was.

Earlier in the morning, UNID had received reports of a secondary lab Peter Albright occasionally used for his personal projects. It hadn't been swept yet by the primary investigation team, but they had their hands full at the Potomac, so Quinn's team was dispatched.

When their car dropped them off in front of the lab, Elena walked past the yellow caution tape without even pausing. She didn't flash a badge at the security staff or explain why they were there. She just pretended like she belonged, so they assumed she did. Quinn followed behind her, feigning the same confidence, with the rest of the interns in tow.

The lab was blinding. The walls, the floors, the tables—they were all so starkly white that the bright daylight bounced off the surfaces. But as they moved into the belly of the building and away from the windows, Quinn appreciated that the reflected light added to the meager light of their flashlights.

"Albright's office is downstairs," Elena said. She was out in front of the team, leading the way, her flashlight swinging back and forth in front of her as they entered the facility. "Oliver and I will scope it out."

Gretchen looked put off.

"Any objections, De Vries?" Elena stared her down for a tense moment, then nodded. "I didn't think so. I want Lehi and Pillay to lift the security footage and search badge access records on the doors. De Vries and Evans can see to the lab. It's room 112, I believe." She looked bored with the whole matter. "Let's just find what we need and get back to headquarters to analyze."

As soon as Elena and Oliver were out of earshot, Gretchen began to protest the assignments. "If anything, Finn should have gone with Oliver. How the heck is he supposed to help me in the lab?"

"Maybe Albright scribbled down some notes in Latin about his travel plans?" Finn quipped.

"I'm just saying that if Elena is going to lead us, she needs to keep her personal relationship out of her decision-making."

"If you have a problem with it, you could get on the com line and tell her what you think," Finn suggested, tossing Quinn a grin as he tried to stir up trouble. "Or you could just tell Hart."

Quinn could tell he was just trying to get Gretchen to shut up for a while. She felt the same. Finn waved bye to Quinn as she and Luan broke off and headed up the stairs to the security offices. Luan sighed loudly in relief.

"I know. She's awful, huh?" Quinn said, watching her footing on the dark stairs.

Luan nodded.

"Very shrill. Not like you, buddy."

He smiled and opened the door to Security.

"You want to take care of access records, and I'll grab the surveillance footage?"

He shrugged and made his way into one of the offices. Quinn took out a power pack and plugged in one of the terminals. One of the hardest parts of this investigation was that as soon as they left the UNID campus, they were without power. IT was providing the teams with power packs, but they could only do so much.

Once she was sure this was the device that stored the surveillance footage, she powered it back down. Then she opened the machine and pulled the hard drive out. Unfortunately, there wasn't enough power to wait for a full copy to complete. She packed it away in an evidence container and met back up with Luan. His data set was much smaller, so he was waiting for a copy to be made. It was just finishing when a voice broke in on the com line.

"Everyone get down to the lab," Finn said, his voice shaky. "We found blood and a bullet hole in the wall."

Luan's eyes widened.

"We'll be right there," Quinn said.

HAVING THE ROOKIES gather up a few files and notes was one thing, but once Headquarters heard about real evidence being found at the lab, UNID forensic teams were swarming the building.

They'd spent hours trying not to get in the way, but not knowing if they should leave. Eventually, a senior agent had snapped at them to get back to HQ. Gretchen seemed pleased with herself on the way home—as if her ballistics expertise had been so useful in identifying what was clearly a bullet hole. Quinn wasn't the only one annoyed in the car. Elena had snapped at her to shut up more than once on the way back.

By the time they arrived back at HQ, the shared case logs were blowing up with new findings. The blood in the lab matched Laycomb's. Someone had shot him in Albright's lab. Quinn tried not to think about how she had been standing where a man had died. Her stomach had turned the whole way back to her dorm.

The day had been exhausting, and she climbed in bed knowing she'd be asleep in seconds.

The hard drive!

Her eyes snapped open, and she scrambled over to her backpack. In the container was all the video surveillance from Albright's lab. Technically, she should have turned it over to the senior team when they had arrived, but she had completely forgotten about it the moment she saw the bright blood marring the pristine laboratory walls.

Sighing loudly, she started to pull her shoes on, but then paused.

Very likely, the answer was on this hard drive. But what if when she turned it in, the evidence was classified beyond her clearance, and then she never knew what happened to Laycomb and Albright? She could look at it now before anyone above her assigned a classification to it. It wasn't the best approach to handling evidence, but no one had taken the assignment from her, and as of right now, she was still in charge of analyzing the videos.

She settled back into her bed with her data-pad and connected it to the hard drive. She dug her headphones out of her nightstand and hooked them up.

Finding the day in question, she backtracked to what the forensic team had reported as Laycomb's time of death. Most of the videos had nothing. They just showed an empty lab for hours and hours. This much surveillance footage would take a whole team a week to watch. It was only a day, but it was twenty-four hours from a hundred different angles and locations.

This was foolish. She'd go to sleep and hand it over in the morning.

She was almost ready to give up when she saw movement in the East Wing hallway.

Laycomb rushed by the camera, and Quinn gasped loudly. She wrote down the time, and looked for Albright's lab footage, but it wasn't there. It didn't exist. A quick glance at the case file told her why. His project was classified. The security officers didn't have a high enough clearance to see what he was working on, so there were no cameras in the lab. She sighed and clicked back into the hallway to watch him walk by again.

Who killed you, Laycomb? And why?

She wished she knew. She fast-forwarded through the footage to see if Laycomb ever came back out, as if she didn't know the answer. It was wishful thinking for her to hope he would leave when she knew he'd been shot.

She was watching the door to the lab so intently she almost missed someone else walking calmly up the hallway toward the surveillance camera. It was a woman, tall and primly dressed. Not a hair was out of place. This was huge. This woman was probably Laycomb's killer. They had her on video. They'd be able to find her and solve this whole case.

She stepped closer to the camera, and Quinn's heart broke.

It was her mother.

No.

She rubbed her eyes and tried to see someone different, but there was no denying it was Karyn Lehi.

Her mom didn't go into the door that Laycomb had disappeared behind. She stopped short of the lab and entered another hallway.

Quinn was still staring at the screen as the minutes ticked away, trying to figure out why her mother had been there and why she hadn't told the investigation team.

A gun fired. It was so loud that for a second, Quinn thought it had been in her building. She tore her earbuds out of her ears as tears started running freely.

SHE MUST HAVE LAIN there for hours. She'd rewatched the video a dozen times. Then she tried following her mother through the facility, but wherever she was going wasn't part of the surveillance layout because eventually she disappeared down a stairwell, and after that Quinn lost track of her. But, in every video, the end result was the same. Her mother would walk off screen, and fifteen minutes later, the gun would fire. A little while later her mother would appear on the ground floor. She'd emerge from a freight elevator and would calmly exit the building.

It didn't make any sense.

Why would her mother push so hard for the investigation if all the evidence led right back to her? Did she think she would be so far above suspicion that she didn't need to cover her tracks?

Quinn lay in her room at four in the morning and tried to quieten her mind. She knew her mother wouldn't have done this. She couldn't have. She loved this world, loved serving and protecting it.

The video was wrong. Someone must have tampered with it.

If it had been anyone else, she would have turned her findings over to the senior team and let the culprit rot away their years in prison, but she wouldn't betray her mother.

Nothing in life was ever definitive, and when it inexplicably was—when all the threads to a mystery tied into a neat little bow with ease—you could be almost certain it was by design. Someone wanted her mother to go down for the power grid failure and Laycomb's murder, and that someone had gone to great lengths to make the case against her airtight.

She threw on some shoes and shoved the hard drive back in her backpack. She would have to bury everything she had found, and she didn't have very long to do it. By morning, the senior investigation team would realize that the surveillance drive was missing and undoubtedly come knocking on her door.

She would do what she could, but she knew deep in her gut that eventually someone else would find the clues that incriminated her mother. They would piece together what she had, and Karyn Lehi would be arrested.

Quinn just needed to find the person who framed her mom before it got that far.

SHE FLOATED THROUGH the morning in a haze.

"Watch it!" Hart called out.

Elena's foot whirled up from the ground. Quinn stepped back quickly, taking the brunt of the kick to her shoulder. Elena had nearly taken her head off.

Hart blew his whistle. "Hit the showers, Lehi. You can try the drill again when your head is in the game."

Quinn started to protest, but surprisingly the usual flare of disappointment was absent.

She always needed to be the best, to prove to her peers she belonged among them, but she shuffled to the locker room without a word. The thought of her mother being thrown in jail consumed her.

It had been twelve hours since she'd found the video, and so far, she had already committed a felony by tampering with crime scene evidence. She'd found the most recent rolling blackout that had hit Albright's lab and then deleted everything on the video that followed. UNID would think the power failure had damaged the surveillance system; it was something that would be easily accepted by the intel teams. Hundreds of hours of evidence had been washed away with the click of a button.

But she wasn't crazy, she'd made a full copy. While she had been tempted to delete the videos altogether, she couldn't stomach the idea of completely destroying them. And she figured that with her luck, just when she deleted them, it would turn out to be the one thing that would absolve her mother. That's how it always happened on television, at least. She'd seen enough late-night episodes of *Agent Anderson: Assassin Spy* to know how these things normally played out.

She rushed through her shower and jogged back to the office. She could use this time to sort through the files on her mother without the other interns looking over her shoulder.

After she'd buried the complete copy of the footage deep in the sharedrive the night before, she had covered up her access records, so they wouldn't wonder why she'd been in the deepest parts of the archives. She figured the Vancouver Incident was old enough that it was rarely referenced by investigation teams, and the files were so massive that a few new folders titled with alpha-numeric gibberish would go unnoticed.

Her paranoia grew as she dug into the old archive to pull up the videos. In the beginning, the office had seemed so welcoming. Despite her peers, she had felt at home at her terminal. It was like she was made to navigate these screens, made to do this job. But now she was on edge, just waiting for someone to jump out of the shadows and accuse her of concealing evidence and abetting a criminal.

She zoomed and enhanced the image, but the blurry figure was still Karyn Lehi. Quinn had watched the video enough now that she didn't even jump when the shot boomed. Then, as the security staff on the footage struggled to secure the area and figure out what had happened, her mother slinked out calmly from the elevator. Her up-do was as prim as always, and, Quinn noted with a grimace, her clothing was just bulky enough to hide a gun. She calmly walked away from a murder scene, her shoes clicking against the white floors of the facility. It was the same click Quinn had heard on Saturday mornings after her mom had made waffles and before she had to rush out the door to save the world.

Quinn wiped a tear from her cheek angrily.

When she heard the door to the office open behind her, she tapped on the key panel quickly. The video disappeared, and in an instant, she was out of the archive.

"Surprise, surprise. Q is misusing her excused absence from PTs to *work*," a voice said behind her.

She spun in her chair and raised an eyebrow at Finn. She was anxious but assured herself there was no way he could have seen what had been on the screen.

"What's the deal?" Finn said, sinking tiredly into his rolling chair and walking it over to her.

"This case is exhausting. Nothing but dead ends and more questions," Quinn lied, hating to break his trust this early in their relationship.

"You know what usually works for me when I'm worn out? A nice, quiet night in," Finn said, stretching lazily. "When's the last time you spent a night just relaxing? No training or sneaking back to your computer."

Quinn rubbed her eyes, trying not to glare at Finn. Quite obviously, there were far greater things to worry about than cozying up with a good book and a cup of tea.

"I need to—"

"You need to take care of yourself. All of UNID is working on this case. It's not your sole burden to bear, Q."

She sighed. She couldn't tell him about her mother, which meant he would never understand that she *was* in this alone. She'd have to go along with it.

"Tell you what—since no one ever taught you how to relax, I'll come by your room tonight. We can watch a movie, and you can forget about all this stuff for a while. How does that sound?"

It sounded like a total waste of time. Maddening.

"That would be perfect," Quinn said.

If Finn noticed how forced her enthusiasm was, he didn't say thing, and a few moments later, the rest of the interns filtered in from the hall.

Elena took charge from the moment she entered the room. "The crime scene is supposed to be open to us later this evening. Until then, let's go over the new field reports and put together a suspect list," she barked at the rest of them. Though it seemed impossible, Elena appeared to be even more uptight than usual.

"Albright worked with Laycomb on the new grid implementation, and Albright is still missing. I don't think it's too far-fetched to think Albright was the one who killed him, right?" Gretchen said.

Luan grunted and shook his head.

"Yes, Pillay? Did you have something to add?" Elena asked, writing Albright's name on the whiteboard. When she was met only with silence, she turned toward him, a tightened fist at her side.

Luan looked back blankly before glancing around the room at the others. Finn jumped in.

"What my mate over here is trying to say is that Albright's office was trashed in the crime scene photos. He's a victim. All his notes were gone, but his wallet was still in his desk. If he were on the run, he would have probably thought to take some money with him."

Luan nodded.

"And they were both part of the project, but didn't necessarily work together," Elena said. "I mean, Albright worked under the inventor, Calenbert. The two of them were all theory. Laycomb was the chief engineer, so he was more on the execution side."

"I'm sure they chatted once or twice," Gretchen said.

"I think one of the things we need to consider is access. Who had access to the lab? That list is very short," Elena said, blatantly ignoring the other girl.

"Well, there's the scientists, the janitorial staff, administrators on the GPP project and with the federal government agencies, the presidential cabinet and all of their security staff, and then a whole slew of congressional ambassadors," Oliver read off. "Hell, even some UNID folks can get into that building. And just because someone isn't on this list doesn't mean they couldn't have stolen a badge or piggybacked on someone else's entry."

"So which badges were scanned that day?" Elena asked.

Quinn let them toss names around for a while. She could have contributed and pulled a name out of thin air, but she didn't want to waste their time when she knew who was there before the gunshot went off. Her mother was the one with the K pin that matched Laycomb's. She was the one who had spoken with his admin the night he went missing. Her mother was in the building, but unaccounted for, when the gun fired.

Elena's marker was poised over the white board.

"Lehi," Oliver said.

Quinn jumped to attention, staring at the rest of the interns.

How did they know? What had they seen? How could her mother already be on their short list of suspects when Quinn had hidden everything? Her breath came in quick bursts. It was all over. They knew.

"Lehi," he repeated, "are you planning on contributing today or what?"

Her brain stuttered to catch up with the conversation. Oh, that's right. The badge records. Luan was looking at her, waiting for her to recount the analysis he'd emailed to her.

"Well, it was the weekend. Everyone who badged into the building had a reason to be there and only accessed the authorized areas."

"But someone could have broken in during the blackout, right? The doors are magnetic. They would have unlocked briefly," Gretchen said.

"Security manually locks them down when that happens," Oliver said.

"There's only one security officer on the weekend though, and six entry points. While he's walking around the facility locking doors, someone could have slipped in through one he hadn't made it to," Gretchen volleyed back.

Elena sighed loudly and pinched the bridge of her nose. "So, the suspect list includes everyone again. Just perfect."

"What about the surveillance cameras?" Finn said. "Did they turn up anything of note?"

Quinn put her best mask on and lied to him. "No, it was a dead end." *It wasn't.* "I turned it in to the senior investigation team, but from what I hear all the footage from the time of the murder was missing." *Because she had deleted it.* "They think the blackouts damaged the surveillance system."

Elena huffed loudly. "Looks like we're going back to the crime scene. Let's be ready to head out in twenty. I want to be there when they open it back up."

"They have better teams than us on the case. What's the point?" Oliver said.

"You're right. Why don't you and Gretchen stay behind? You're both useless anyway," Elena's voice rattled.

Quinn glanced around, noting for the first time how tense it was in the room. She'd been so wrapped up in her own inner turmoil she hadn't noticed how Elena's unpleasantness seemed more hurt than angry. Where she normally stood proud and tall, today she was slumped forward. Her dark brown hair, which was always in a perfect bun high atop her head was sticking out in all directions.

Oh.

She'd thought whatever Elena and Oliver had was just a fling, but the Russian princess was obviously more invested than Quinn had realized.

Elena grabbed her coat and stomped out of the room.

Oliver turned back to his computer, and Gretchen looked more pleased than usual.

The room was so tense Quinn had to stop herself from running out of it.

"LET'S SPLIT UP. WE'LL recheck the access points," Finn suggested. The traitor grabbed Luan by the sleeve, and they disappeared toward the west side of the building.

Rude.

They could have sent Luan with the princess, but since Elena didn't complain, neither did she.

This morning, all she could think about was her mother, but now her mind was loud with a different matter entirely. It urged her to apologize. She'd known Oliver was messing around with Gretchen, but other than thinking it was a good piece of gossip, she hadn't thought to pass that information along.

"Petrova," Quinn started, "I'm sorry about Oliver—"

"Oh, come on," Elena snapped, looking uncomfortable. "I don't need your pity, Lehi, and if I wanted your opinion, I would have asked for it."

Quinn tried again. "You were right about them, though. They really are useless."

"As if your boy-toy is much better," Elena said, turning a corner sharply and walking faster up the long stretch of the hallway toward the lab.

Quinn scoffed. "Excuse me? Finn has been part of this investigation every step of the way. He's a part of this team."

"He's dead weight." Elena slowed her brisk pace and spun around. "Surely you've noticed."

Quinn shook her head.

"All of his successes are from your hard work, Lehi. You two aren't a team," Elena spat, looking bitter. "He's a parasite, and he's using you."

Quinn felt like she had been punched in the gut. "You're wrong."

"I'm just trying to open your eyes to what is right in front of you," Elena said, continuing on in the direction of the lab. "You don't have to listen, but don't come crying to me when he blindsides you."

"Why would I ever come crying to *you*?" Quinn was mad, and before she knew it, she was lashing out. "Why don't you stay out of my relationship with Finn? It's none of your business, and I hardly think I should take advice from someone who—"

She suddenly realized where they were.

They were down the hall from Lab 112. They were where her mother had been on the tape.

"Someone who what? Tell me, Lehi. Go ahead. Just say it," Elena demanded.

Quinn ignored her, tearing down the hallway her mom had disappeared into.

"Lehi, wait up!" Elena called out behind her.

Quinn wove through the halls with far more familiarity than she should have had. Her flashlight bounced off the walls as she followed the path her mother had taken on the camera. Eventually she came to the staircase that descended down into the basement level of the facility. Her mother had disappeared into the depths of the building, and before Quinn hadn't been able to follow, but now she could. The basement was a far cry from the shiny surfaces above ground. The air was damp, with cinder blocks and bare bulbs lining the corridors. Past some janitorial closets and the freight elevator Quinn recognized as her mother's escape route, she saw an office that had been roped off by the initial investigation team. She ducked under the tape and stepped in, Elena at her heels.

She recognized this place immediately from the photographs.

"Ugh, I hate this place," Elena said.

That's right. When they had come to the facility before to look around, Elena had investigated Albright's office.

They had taken pictures and gathered up all of the papers that had been strewn around. All of Albright's scribbles had been scanned and saved on the sharedrive.

"Look, we checked this place top to bottom, and then the follow-up team checked behind us. I know you're not a fan of Oliver, but we were thorough."

This was where her mother was when the gun went off. At least this absolved her of the murder, but why was she talking to Albright? What business did she have with him?

Quinn sat down at his desk and tried to imagine it from his point of view. Her mom tore into the office in hurry, she opened her mouth, and she said what? Or did she say nothing at all?

The investigation team was under the impression that Albright was either involved in the crimes being committed or he himself had been kidnapped. Was her mom onto him? Or had she been the one who had taken him? And who had destroyed his office? Was it her mother as she tranquilized him and hauled his body somewhere, or had Albright been enraged at having been caught?

Quinn shook her head. No. Her mother left alone on the footage.

Quinn opened his desk drawer and prowled around his stuff.

"Lehi! Put on some freakin' gloves!" Elena cried out, pulling gloves out of her jacket and shoving them at Quinn.

Quinn jerked them on quickly before going back to rummaging through his drawers.

"Ugh. I wanted to check out the lab, but here I am in smelly's office again," Elena whined, skimming the titles on Albright's immense bookshelves to occupy herself.

What Quinn saw next made her stomach turn. Among his paperclips and staple refills was a familiar golden pin. It wasn't the same as her mother's in the photo in her office, but it was close. Her mother rarely wore yellow gold, so she would have noticed that when she saw the picture.

She held the pin in her palm and tried to not let her mind spin out of control, but the conclusion was clear.

Her mother wasn't there to stop Albright.

She was affiliated with him and Laycomb. She was helping Albright. Quinn was starting to side with Oliver. Peter Albright was a suspect, and as much as she tried to deny it, her mother was starting to look like one, too.

SHE'D STAYED QUIET during the car ride home and had barely remembered her date with Finn until he'd taken her hand and led her back to her room.

She just wanted to be alone. She didn't want him to see her like this because every ounce of her felt like it was going to break apart. She'd tried so hard to prove her mother innocent, but she'd only found more evidence against her.

Finn loaded up a movie on her data-pad and leaned against the headboard of her bed. She laid her head on his shoulder and tried to watch the movie, but her mind was reeling.

After twenty minutes of her shuffling every other moment, Finn spoke up, "Relax, Q, please."

"I'm sorry," she said. "I have trouble turning my brain off. I'll be right back." Quinn went into her bathroom and shut the door behind her. She needed to get herself together and pause her investigation for tonight. All of the facts of the case were jumbled in her mind, but she knew everything would be clearer in the morning.

When she came back in to her bedroom, Finn was hunched over her data-pad, swiping through screens quickly.

"What are you doing?" she asked.

His head snapped up in her direction. "Just looking at the case log. Seeing if anything has been added."

She took the pad from his hands and glanced at the recent activity. "No, that's not what you were doing."

Finn looked nervous.

"You were looking at my private files. Why are you snooping?"

"I just thought that if I knew what was going on with you, I could help," he said.

"Then why wouldn't you just ask?"

"Can we just drop it?" He looked outwardly embarrassed, but deep in his eyes, there was a flare of anger.

Part of her wanted to push for more answers, but she decided to give him some mercy.

Finn was quiet for a minute, and then he asked, "What did you and Elena find?"

"We told you in the car. There was nothing new in Albright's office or the lab."

"I guess it doesn't matter anyway," he said, still miffed.

"What do you mean?"

"This case keeps going nowhere. We have no solid suspects, little forensics to go on, and until Peter Albright resurfaces, I'd say UNID can do little more than twiddle its thumbs."

"Oh," she said, deflating.

"I don't think Luan is a threat, by the way. I was thinking about it today. He's smart, but they aren't going to hire someone who won't even talk to them. I prodded him for an opinion all day, but only got grunts and shrugs out of him."

"He would be a valuable asset to the agency. He just needs to be placed on the right team," Quinn said.

"Oliver and Gretchen are hardly up to the task," he continued, ignoring her comment. "The director won't advance someone who doesn't show up for the investigation and is always missing from the meetings."

"Yeah."

"And Elena? Hart saw how unprofessional she acted over Lee. I'd say she's out of the running now."

"Elena's a strong competitor. I just think Oliver really hurt her. She's not made of stone; she was heartbroken."

"She shouldn't have started anything up with a co-worker."

Quinn blinked. "We're seeing each other. What's the difference?"

Finn smiled. "The difference is that we aren't flaunting it in front of everyone. We're discreet."

"So, you're saying I'll win?"

He held her eyes for a moment, and she saw it again. The anger from before mixed with a cold calculating look that made her stomach drop.

Finn laughed. "No, Quinn. That's not what I'm saying."

She thought back to her conversation with Elena at the lab and felt like a fool for not seeing it before. "You're saying that you're going to win."

"Look," he started, "you're great...and lovely. I've really enjoyed getting to know you, but they aren't going to pick you either, Q."

She hadn't caught him trying to figure out what was wrong with her. He'd been snooping for her leads.

"Why?"

"Your mother is the director. They don't need a nepotism scandal; it already looks like your mother is mismanaging the hell of out the agency. Not only is she helpless to stop the attack on the grid, but she's also hiring her family to be part of the failing intelligence team? That's hardly a way to make it better. And if they do pick you? All someone has to do to make them reconsider is file a grievance with the board; Elena is sure to do that. They'll look at all the other candidates, and they'll see me: a shining example of a star employee, tried and tested by the intern program, and part of every accomplishment made these few weeks. It'll be an easy choice."

"What about the other job? The one at International that you want more than UNID?"

"I changed my mind," he said with a nonchalance he couldn't quite pull off.

"You used me," she said quietly.

"No, doll. I didn't. I just know how this is going to play out. I'm doing you a favor telling you now," Finn said, reaching over and patting her on the knee. "Now you can prepare yourself for it. So you won't be disappointed."

She already was disappointed.

In him.

In what she'd hoped for them.

In herself for not seeing him moving chess pieces all along.

When Finn left, she didn't cry. She wasn't heartbroken; she was just mad. She pulled Albright's 'K' pin out of her pocket and glared at the door. Finn might think he'd already won, but tomorrow, she was busting this case wide open.

8

"DIRECTOR, MAY I HAVE a minute?"

She showed up at seven sharp. Karyn hated early unscheduled meetings.

Her mother looked sternly at her before her eyes softened. Quinn knew why.

She'd pulled her hair into a high ponytail and brushed back all her flyaways. Her pony had swung behind her like a whip the whole way across the UNID campus. Right now it was the only difference between her and her mother, because today she had dressed in her most director-y pantsuit, she had applied her makeup with the utmost precision, and then she had pinned Albright's 'K' to her lapel.

"Shut the door," the director commanded.

Quinn followed her orders and then took a seat across from her mother, holding her chin high. The ball was in her court now.

"Where did you get that?" Karyn asked.

"Oh, this? I found it in Peter Albright's office. I thought it was odd. I've only ever seen women wear jewelry with an initial on it, and I've yet to see a K in his name. But now that I think about it, I've seen you wear something similar; so, I thought I'd follow your lead. After all, Albright won't mind if I borrow it since he's missing."

"Quinn, you need to drop this—"

"No, Mom. You need to explain some things to me. Last week, I saw you on a surveillance tape of the east wing of Albright's lab. Seconds before Laycomb died, you were slinking around a facility you had no business in. Can you explain that to me?"

Karyn took a long moment, face schooled and blank. "We've talked about this, Quinn. I'm leading the investigation effort. It is hardly strange for me to interview key personnel."

"Sure, but I would think it's a breach of protocol for you to not report being in the facility at the time of Laycomb's death—that you were in Albright's office. This is the second time I've caught you hiding your involvement in this case. It seems to me like you didn't want anyone to know you were there because maybe what you were doing there wasn't entirely on the up and up—"

"Excuse me?"

"Tell me, Director Lehi. Tell me how you even got into the facility. Your badge was never scanned. Or maybe the power just conveniently went off when you needed to sneak in like a ghost. Maybe you knew the path the security officer would have taken to lock the doors down."

"Quinn."

The door opened behind her, and Quinn continued glowering at her mother with her back to the newcomer.

"Director Lehi," her mother's assistant started, "a car is here to take you to Vice President Gamble's office. They say it's urgent."

"Of course," her mother said, standing and gathering her briefcase.

Her assistant left the room, and her mother turned to her. "This isn't what it looks like, Quinn. I promise. I don't have time to explain it to you now, but everything I've done has been to protect this world and its people."

Quinn's lip quivered. Everything her mother was saying echoed the things she believed about her. But was it true, or was Quinn being manipulated for the second time in a few short weeks?

"You have until the end of the day, Director. I want an explanation, or I'm going to distribute my findings to the investigation teams." Quinn stood tall and held her head high before marching out of her mother's office without another word.

She took her pin off in the elevator and shoved it into her pocket.

She was due at the intern office at eight, but part of her wanted to crawl back in bed until her mother summoned her and begged for mercy. She was a horrible daughter, but maybe her mother wasn't so great either.

She spent the first hour of the workday avoiding any conversations with Finn and reading the available evidence for the case. It was hardly interesting. All the juicy bits of detail were hidden in the archives away from prying eyes. Still, what else was she supposed to do until her mother explained herself?

Eventually, after her eyes started to glaze over the case log she had read hundreds of times, she clicked into the gallery. Of course, there were crime scene photos, some of which had been taken at the shore of the Potomac; she wished she hadn't seen those. There were blueprints of buildings and schematics of the solar towers that connected the grid. Finally, there was a set of images that made her pause because they looked so familiar. Everyone was dressed up for a party, smiling for the camera.

Why did she recognize these?

She pulled up the entire album and looked at the description. The images were taken by the *Globe Daily* at President Camden's GPP event at the White House. She'd seen the album before on her first case at UNID in which upper-level bankers had attended the party during the theft of the Starlight Diamond.

UNID's classification system had picked it up because of the GPP tags.

She opened a query and searched.

Laycomb, Henry.

No results were returned. You would think he would have attended the event, but if they had caught a glimpse of it, the facial recognition hadn't managed to pick it up.

She searched again.

Albright, Peter.

The system returned one image. Peter Albright smiled for the camera with an older man with white hair and a goatee. The goateed man was frowning and looked put off at having his picture taken. Below the picture was the older man's name: Martin Kozlov.

"Who's Martin Kozlov?" Quinn said aloud.

"Seriously?" Elena said.

Quinn winced. She hadn't meant to voice her question, and now Elena was looking at her like she was an idiot.

"He's in this picture with Albright," Quinn explained.

Elena rolled her eyes. "Of course he is. Kozlov was one of the lead engineers on the GPP. He worked for Laycomb on the engineering side of the implementation."

"Has anyone checked in on him? Laycomb and Albright are connected by GPP. Shouldn't we look into all the lead scientists who were involved?" Quinn said.

"Uhhh, I think they did." Wheeling over to Quinn's station, Elena tapped through the case file until she got to a folder marked "Resolved Leads" and opened a set of interview notes.

Quinn read aloud, "Calenbert, who developed the early stages of the technology, is in retirement on an island in the Pacific. Interviewers made contact with Martin Kozlov the day of the disappearances. He has refused to be involved with the investigation but wishes the team the best in finding his colleagues."

"See? He's safe and sound."

"Hart," Quinn called out, "do you mind if I grab some fieldies and go look into Kozlov?"

Her beefy supervisor shrugged. "Sure. Take someone with you though."

Finn glanced at her, but she pointedly ignored him.

"What do you say, Petrova? Want to go talk to an engineer? It might be useful to have someone there who can speak his language," Quinn said, hoping the linguistics shot didn't go over Finn's head.

Elena shrugged and grabbed her data-pad.

When Quinn located them, Riya and Miguel didn't seem too put out at the impromptu assignment.

"What's with the princess? Where's your boy scout?" Riya asked as they climbed into one of the black surveillance vans.

"It didn't work out," Quinn said, opening up the back doors to climb in.

Riya frowned but didn't press further.

To Elena's credit, she didn't say "I told you so." She just strapped in to the seat beside Quinn and pulled up the record they had on Kozlov.

MARTIN KOZLOV LIVED alone. He didn't have any pets, and from his file, it didn't seem like he was very close with his family. He had divorced his wife twenty years ago, and she had moved to Nebraska with their children. He'd had limited contact with them ever since.

Riya had joked the whole way over that she was going to kick in his door, but when they got there, she just knocked.

Kozlov opened the door enough that the chain lock on his side pulled taut. He didn't seem happy to have company. As soon as he saw their black suits and sunglasses, he grumbled, "I have already told you people what I know."

"We had some follow-up questions," Miguel said calmly. "Mind if we come in, Dr. Kozlov?"

Unchaining the door, Kozlov growled, "Like I have a choice."

Papers were stacked all over his house. Scribblings of formulas and sketches of schematics had been penciled on the walls. He looked every bit the stereotypical mad scientist, with white hair that stuck out on either side of his head and a goatee in serious need of a trim. He led them to the living room and plopped down in an armchair.

Miguel sat in the other armchair. Riya moved some of the notebook paper that littered his couch to a coffee table, and she and

Quinn took a seat. Elena looked positively uncomfortable with the whole situation. She grimaced as she sank down next to them.

"First of all, Dr. Kozlov, I would like to extend the agency's condolences. I'm sure someone has reached out to you regarding Dr. Laycomb's passing," Quinn said.

"Pulled him out of the river," Kozlov said unceremoniously. "Doesn't surprise me. Henry wasn't a very good swimmer."

Quinn blinked, a little taken aback at how casual he was about his colleague's death. She took a moment and then continued, "I'm sure the interviewers who came before us also mentioned that Peter Albright is missing."

"Yeah," he said.

"Are you close with Peter?" Riya asked.

"He was a good kid, but no. Can't say I was."

"Martin," Quinn leaned forward and held eye contact with him. "Do you know what's going on with the power grid? Do you know why very bad things are happening to the scientists who worked on the project?"

He shrugged. "No, I don't."

She swallowed hard before asking the one question she'd come here for, "Are you worried someone might come for you next?"

Kozlov smiled. "No, I'm not."

There was a sinking feeling in Quinn's stomach at the look on Martin's face. He knew something.

"Why aren't you worried?" Elena asked.

"I think we're done here," Kozlov said. "I'm tired."

As he showed them the door, Quinn looked at the old man and felt her veins turn to steel. "I read in your file that you don't get many visitors, sir. Just know that that's about to change. You and I are friends now. I'll be around, Kozlov."

He glared at her.

"The grid failure isn't just people sitting in the dark and not getting to watch television. The world is suffering. There are people out there who are dying, and it's only going to get worse," she said. "If you know something and you aren't telling us, then you are killing them. I hope you realize that."

The engineer's eyes softened a little, and then he slammed the door in their faces.

SHE WAS SITTING IN the director's armchair, tapping her foot impatiently when her mother returned from her meeting with the Vice President. She didn't know what could have kept her there so late, but from the look on Karyn's face, it had been one hell of a day.

"Martin Kozlov knows something," Quinn said.

"Do you have any evidence?" her mom asked, sinking tiredly into her seat.

"Just a hunch."

Karyn smiled. "Hunches are good. Keep following it."

Quinn nodded, Albright's pin clinking as she placed it on her mom's desk, and then she waited. Her mom owed her answers, and she was here to collect.

The director sighed. "The 'K' stands for Kaosa. I used to be a member. I'm not anymore."

"And Albright?"

"He was an old friend. I really did go to his lab to talk to him about the GPP's failure. I was in the basement, Quinn. Albright wasn't even there. I never heard the gunshot, and by the time I left, I knew how bad it would look if I said I had been there. There was no way I could save them if I was in jail."

"What is Kaosa?"

"When I was a part of it, it was just an organization of government employees who wanted to make the world better. We wanted to help people. The old grids we were on were faulty, and natural disasters could take them out for weeks. We didn't feel it a lot in D.C., but citizens all over the world suffered from major blackouts. We needed a power solution to propel us into the future. People like Laycomb and Albright were researching solutions. People like me were helping keep the world afloat until they could fix everything."

"So why did you quit?"

Karyn shook her head, looking sad. "Some of the ideas floating to the top were getting out of hand. They wanted to build their own facility...their own army. I wouldn't be a part of that."

"Promise me you had nothing to do with the grid failure—nothing to do with Laycomb's murder and Albright's disappearance. Please, Mom."

"I promise," she said, as sincere as Quinn had ever seen her.

And Quinn believed her. She'd keep the evidence buried, and maybe one day, when the power came back on, she would delete it. Until then, she was going to follow her hunch about Martin Kozlov; one day, she'd break him.

9

THE MURDER OF DR. LAYCOMB and the disappearance of Dr. Albright took highest priority for days, and then it was discovered that President Camden was also MIA. Now, very few people were concerned about the scientists. But, Quinn reasoned, the three cases had to be related, and while everyone else was focused on the President, Quinn felt confident that getting Kozlov to talk would be the clue she needed to solve this. Kozlov, no matter what he said to the contrary, knew something. Which was why she'd been pestering him every week for two months now.

What a horrible two months it had been too.

The power was still out, and things were getting out of control. It hadn't taken long before cars stopped running and every battery died. While a select few government buildings, like UNID and the UN Capitol building, had installed temporary solar units to run all the basics, D.C. itself had become the center of civilian unrest. There were protests, riots, and tent cities popping up everywhere. She almost couldn't blame people for their hysterics. Frankly, she felt more than a little guilty for what she had right now, which wasn't much, but it was a lot more than most.

Anything that was run completely within government servers and networks was usable for them. Satellite feeds? Still good. Closed-loop com systems? Check. But nice-to-have things like live surveillance on civilian property? Not so much. So they still had a lot of capability, but it was far from their normal arsenal of investigative tools. C-SIGs pulled enormous amounts of energy, so they were a luxury that UNID officers could no longer rely upon. That meant they were doing more work by hand. Their options for travel were more limited. Only a small percent of UNID vehicles were allowed to charge, and those were used only for pre-authorized work. So, this morning she'd put in her weekly request for her visit to Martin Kozlov and suffered through the normal cries of favoritism from the other interns who had thus far only submitted personal requests. She'd learned to drown them out.

Quinn did her best to ignore the havoc the past few months had caused as she and Riya made the familiar drive to Kozlov's house. They desperately needed things to go back to normal. Maybe today would be the day he broke.

"So, how do you want to swing the interview this time? Good cop, bad cop? Good cop, good cop? Or," Riya said with a sneaky grin, "my personal favorite—bad cop, bad cop?"

"I think the heartfelt pleas to his humanity are wearing him down."

"Oh really? At what rate? I'm not sure that cantankerous old man can deliver his humanity before we're all trampled beneath hordes of rioters. If that's what we are waiting on, I think this whole thing is a waste of time."

"Who knows? Maybe he'll surprise you."

And me, she thought to herself.

When they parked in front of his house, Riya pulled up over the curb.

"Do you have to park like that?" she asked.

"I don't like taking unnecessary steps. You know my efficiency gene is working one hundred percent of the time."

"I prefer to mind the rules of the road."

"Who's to enforce them right now?" she replied with a smirk, climbing the stairs to Kozlov's landing.

Quinn's first rap on the door made it swing open soundlessly, and she paused, her hand still hovering in the air. She looked to Riya worriedly, but her friend was already pulling out her gun and pushing Quinn behind her.

"Stay close," she whispered, pressing a finger to her lips. They entered the house slowly. Riya methodically checked each room, looking for signs of Kozlov or a struggle. Nothing seemed out of place, but in his office a pile of papers lay on the floor near his desk, scattered as if they'd fallen off the edge.

Quinn picked up the page on top. It was notes—code fragments that didn't seem to amount to anything, and a bunch of terms she didn't understand. Sifting through the pages, there were diagrams of a large machine. The words SI-FIGHTER and Waypoint appeared a couple of times.

"His drawers have been emptied," Riya said, slamming one shut. "He's running."

Quinn stood up, papers in hand, then noticed the screen of his computer. The power light was on.

"There's power!" she said, hurrying to the back of his desk and searching for the source. A battery pack was hooked up to the computer, much like the ones they were currently using in the field.

She tapped the screen to bring it to life. A progress bar displayed "100%" on what she knew was a very pricy nano-code development program.

"He's downloaded something to a nano-drive," she said eagerly.

"Okay, so what was it?" Riya asked, crossing her arms.

"Let's see," Quinn said, tapping out of the download screen. But, just as she clicked on the file folder, the entire system went blank. The hard drive began to smoke and pop. Then silence.

"Damnit!" she shouted.

Riya looked dumbfounded. "What just happened?"

"He set it to self-destruct."

"Unplug it and bring it with us. Maybe we can still salvage it."

Quinn knew it was unlikely, but she packed it up anyway.

Once they got back to HQ they took the evidence straight to the IT lab. Riya and Quinn were then shooed away as the pros went to work on the hard drive.

"Let's go make our report," Riya said. "Hopefully they'll have good news for us when we get back."

Quinn and Riya went straight to Agent Hart after learning Riya's team leader was out sick. He called in the report and instructed the two of them to fill out the details on the case log. Quinn wanted to hurry and finish up. They needed to start looking for Martin right away. He wouldn't have run for nothing, and whatever he had on that nano-drive was important. She just knew it.

It took them about an hour. They were just wrapping up when an announcement came in over the speaker system. "All agents on duty report to the auditorium for an update from the Director."

Their brows rose in unison. Could this be about their find? Or had someone located the president?

The auditorium was noisy. Everyone was speculating as to the reason for the all-hands. Quinn spotted Elena in the crowd, and as soon as their eyes locked, Elena began to push through the crowd to her side.

"What's this all about, Lehi?"

"I have no idea. Contrary to what you think, my mom doesn't share UNID business with me."

"Sure. If you say so," she said.

Her mother stepped onto the stage, and everyone took a seat. "First," she said, looking out over the crowd of agents, "I want to thank everyone for their diligence during this confusing time. Many of you have been working around the clock on our several high-priority cases. We've just received key information I wanted to brief you all on. A terrorist organization that calls itself Kaosa has admitted to, or perhaps I should say, *bragged* about their orchestration of the GPP outage."

The room began to buzz. Whispered confusion flowed through the auditorium. From the chatter, it seemed that no one else was aware of this group. But the name Kaosa sent a tingling chill through Quinn's body.

"We still do not understand the motives of this organization or what they hope to gain, but it is clear from the explicit knowledge they revealed of the GPP system that they had the means to accomplish its destruction. Vice President Gamble has assured me that our best people are working night and day to restore the power. Many of you may not have heard yet, but UNID agents learned today that Dr. Martin Kozlov has disappeared. Inside his home, we recovered classified GPP documents.

"You all know what is happening outside of these walls. The world is falling apart. I'm certain the retrieval of certain scientists with extensive understanding of the system would be instrumental in achieving our goal sooner. Which is why, even though the president's disappearance is still a top priority, I'm asking all divisions to move complete focus to the retrieval of Dr. Albright and Dr. Kozlov. Based on the timing of Kaosa's message and Dr. Kozlov's hasty departure, we believe he was involved in the sabotage of the GPP."

Quinn's face snapped to Riya's beside her. Kozlov? A Kaosa terrorist? Anger surged. She regretted every cajoling smile she'd flashed that backstabbing bastard.

Her mom needed to wrap this little thing up. Her fingers were itching for her keyboard. She was going to find Martin, and he was going to spend the rest of his miserable life in prison.

She was on her feet as soon as her mother stepped away from the lectern. She pushed through the crowd as agents loitered to gossip over the juicy news.

"Excuse us. Girl with a plan coming through," Riya said, shoving people aside as they hurried to the basement, Elena in tow.

"How do you know she has a plan?" Elena asked.

"The look on her face. Do you not recognize it at this point?"

Elena huffed, but Quinn drowned out the noise. She knew exactly what to do. Martin would be hiding. He'd know they still had sat imagery to find him on the run, but what he didn't know what that she'd perfected a way to find someone trying to hide themselves.

She pulled up to her desk and opened the program she'd developed just before starting at UNID.

"What are you doing?" Elena snapped, angry to be in the dark about anything.

Luan stepped through the door just as Quinn began to the enter the first search parameters.

"I'm running a facial recognition program I developed while I was in school. It's bulky, so I can only search one parameter at a time. I've been running searches on our other missing persons but haven't hit anything. I have been thinking they are either being kept somewhere out of satellite view, or dead. But Martin is probably on the move right now; he'll be trying to leave the city, and out in the open, but probably concealing himself to avoid detection. If he's out there, I can find him."

"Alright," Elena said, "shoot us copies. We'll all run parameters at the same time, just tell us what to do."

The three of them stared at her in astonishment.

"Did you just offer to help me?" she asked.

"No. I offered to do my job," she said, crossing her arms, "like I always do."

Quinn shut her still-open mouth. "Uh, okay then. I'm sending it to all of you now."

Elena and Luan pulled up to their stations, and Riya sat beside her at Finn's. They all got to work, running the searches one at a time, but moving through them quickly. The satellite images flashed quick as bullets from an automatic weapon across their screens, looking from every angle, making controlled and modified calculations. Hours ticked by as they cycled through over sixty parameters. Finn stopped in at one point. He spared a glance at their work, scoffed, and left to get coffee.

It was parameter number sixty-two that dinged with a hit. They all huddled eagerly around Elena's station. There he was. The image was clear, but Martin had attached a full beard and filled his mouth with something that made his cheeks appear bloated. It hardly looked like him, but it was.

"We found him," Elena said in amazement.

"Hey, what's going on?" asked Agent Hart, walking in with Finn and Oliver trailing behind.

Quinn's heart nearly thudded to a stop. They'd found him, but it was Elena's terminal. She'd get this win. She opened her mouth ready to object.

"Quinn found Kozlov," Elena said. "We were working off her program, and it hit."

Quinn couldn't believe her ears. Elena had just given her the credit. Had she ever known this woman?

Finn piped into the silence of Elena's shocking statement. "I was working this project too. Just left to grab a little caffeine."

Luan stood up to his full bear-sized height. "Piss off, Evans. You're such a tool."

Finn stammered in embarrassment, and Riya barked out a laugh. "He finally speaks, and what do you know? He's full of wisdom."

"Good work, team. Let's call this in," Hart said, reaching for his com line.

QUINN WALKED INTO HER mom's office, still high on her win, but knowing what she needed to do now.

She'd proven a lot to herself these past few months. She would make an excellent agent. She was smart, tougher than she'd thought possible, and coincidentally in the best shape of her life. But, if nothing else, these months had taught her that her mom was right. She might have won over a few people she'd worked with closely every day, but she wouldn't be able to do that with every agent in UNID. People were going to think poorly of her. Worse—they would lose respect for her mother, and the world needed Karyn Lehi at the helm. They needed someone who could get this job done, which was why she was going to turn down the offer she'd just received.

She knocked on the door to her mom's office. *Maybe for the last time*, she thought to herself.

"Come in," her mom called from the other side.

Her mother was shrugging on her bulletproof vest and was decked head-to-toe in full tactical gear. Quinn hadn't seen her in this get-up in over a year.

"Mom, what are you doing?"

"There's a helo waiting on the roof. I'm going to apprehend Dr. Kozlov, and it's all thanks to your excellent investigative skills," she said with a smile that lit up the room.

"But—you don't go into the field anymore," she said in confusion.

"Director Lehi didn't, but Senior Agent Lehi does."

"What? You got demoted?! They can't do that. I'm not taking the job. I'll find something else."

"The hell you will, Quinn. I didn't get demoted; I resigned. I'm staying on as the team lead for one of our younger teams. I've always liked training the newbies. But you," she said, pointing at her, "you *will* take that job. We had nothing on this case. But *you* had the hunch about Kozlov. *You* called me out when evidence led to my door. It was *your* program that found him! I was wrong. And you know how much I hate admitting that," she said, as she brought her hand up to cup Quinn's cheek. "You belong here more than anyone. You earned it, and you're taking it. And you know what?"

Quinn shook her head, her eyes misty at the pride that laced her mother's voice and the love in her eyes.

"What?" she asked.

"I'm happy. This is a good thing. Let someone else have this stuffy office. I miss the field."

Quinn reached for her mother, wrapping her arms tightly around her and holding on like she hadn't since she was a little girl.

"Are you sure this agency is big enough for the both of us?" she asked, smiling through fallen tears.

"It'll have to be," her mom replied, stepping away and striding to the door. "Alright, I'm off to—hang on, where is it you spotted him?"

"Sunset. Sunset, South Carolina."

SNEAK PEEK

Find out what happens next in the action-packed full-length novel *Waypoint!*

How far will they go to restore the power?

It's been lights-out for three months and society is already falling into chaos.

Teenage tech-genius Simon Harper and his team of fellow gamers have been searching for the cause of the outage since it went down. Simon and his twin brother West are often at odds, but when the key to restoring power drops into their hands, they'll risk everything and join forces to bring it back.

Descend into an epic, young adult adventure, featuring family and friendship with a heart-skipping side of romance.

Mysterious deaths and disappearances are piling up, and unknown enemies are everywhere. As the brothers make their 500-mile journey to Waypoint they'll have to decide who they can trust because the girls who join them along the way might be allies, or they could be the very enemy they are running from.

★ ★ ★ ★ ★

"Thanks to its tantalizing pace, well-established consequences, and complicated character development, this novel is worth writing home about. **I didn't feel ready for it to end.**" -Independent Book Review

SIMON

THE DARK RED SKY LOOMED above as loose dust from the earth whipped around the Knights of Arcadia. Granules of sand scraped across his B-CLASS visor. His new Regent-issued helmet was dirty, and no amount of rubbing would ever get it clean again. They had upgraded the HUD and improved the tactical lighting instruments but seemed to have forgotten to make the damn things scratchproof. *So much for building an army of super soldiers.*

At this point, Simon would have ripped off his helmet if he didn't think he would suffocate from the poor environmental conditions of the hostile zone. He knew it wasn't time to die yet—not when the enemy was lurking on the horizon. His HUD didn't detect them, but he could feel them out there. They were waiting to pounce. The bastards were trigger-happy and wanted nothing more than the complete annihilation of his military outfit—his friends.

The invaders had started terraforming, filling the air with noxious chemicals. Their drills were digging deep into the earth, pumping in poison like a bee sting. Their foreign technology was saturating underground rivers and ecosystems with toxic venom, eating away at the indigenous life forms.

Scenes had played out in front of Simon in recent months, scenes of children saying goodbye to their childhood homes, families packing up and leaving when they realized this battleground was no place to put down roots. He hoped they had made it far away from all the shooting and sickness.

For him, there was no place else he'd rather be than on the front line with his comrades.

"Listen up," a sharp voice crackled through the com. "We'll approach from the east. Keep a tight formation and try not to push ahead of the group." Collins was their fearless commander. His expectations were always clear and concise, but his disapproval at their failures could be searing.

"It's strange, right?" Simon pondered aloud. "We crossed into enemy territory a few hundred feet back, but there's nothing on the HUD."

"They're waiting for us to make our move," Troy said in his deep register. "Cowards."

Collins sighed. "Don't worry about them. Stick to the plan, and we'll be able to take the Citadel. Everyone in position?"

"Ready when you are," Malachi called out from his vantage point. Simon always felt better knowing Malachi was watching them through the scope of his sniper rifle. His quick reflexes and deadly accuracy had saved their team countless times throughout the years.

"All right, Troy and I are up front," Collins said as he took a step toward the looming structure in the distance. "Oh, and Tucker?"

"Yes, Commander?" the youngest member of their squad responded.

"*So help me* if you try to rush the enemy again. That never works," Collins growled, his hulking form looking tense in the low light of the crimson sky.

"Understood." Tucker sounded sincere, but Simon knew better. The kid had gotten them in messy altercations in recent months, but he was Troy's little brother. Abandoning him to fend for himself with a rookie squad was never even suggested.

Besides, Simon knew a thing or two about dealing with brothers who act first and think later.

He checked his ammunition and preemptively reloaded. It was always better to walk into the hot zone with a full clip. The Knights of

Arcadia trudged forward along the crumbling stone walls, their large, muscular figures moving in surprising soundlessness.

Simon continued to take inventory of their supplies. He had long filled the role of medic on their team. The others had tried their hands at it but were always too frantic in the rushed, desperate moments to make quick choices. The pressure never bothered him. There was something about everything falling apart that made the world go incredibly still. He brought up the rear, hoping one syringe of adrenaline would be enough for what was sure to be a bloody skirmish.

The com lines were eerily devoid of chatter—so much so that Simon kept glancing at the display on his visor to see if his receiver was still operating. He could occasionally hear one of the other men taking an even breath through the constant hiss and crackle of the radio feed.

"Malachi, any sign of them?" Collins's head was on a pivot as the tension grew heavier in the air.

"It's a ghost town. You think they're out there?" Malachi sounded doubtful.

"How the hell am I supposed to know?" Collins snapped back. Their commander was itching for a brawl. Simon could hear it in his voice. Collins craved the bloodshed of a good battle.

Troy chuckled. "Now, now, children. Let's settle down."

"Move your ass. We can't be out here forever," the commander grumbled.

Simon laughed, falling in step with Tucker. The kid was looking down the barrel of his gun, seemingly unaware of his periphery. Simon shook his head and smiled.

He knew there was irony in his joy somewhere. He was content in this decaying world. Somehow it was better than being back home. The problems were solvable; the mission was predictable. The threat of dying a hundred times over seemed better than being helpless.

Troy and Collins approached an intersection up ahead where tall stone walls surrounded a cross of dirt paths.

"Be advised; you're in my blind spot," Malachi said.

"C'mon," Collins said as he pushed forward with Troy at his side.

When Tucker gasped into his radio, Simon felt his stomach sink. He whipped his head around to see the kid break formation and dash toward a flash of metal gleaming in the Arcadian sun.

"Tucker! Don't!" Simon called out. The alluring alien weaponry beckoned Tucker forward into what was sure to be—

The familiar *whisp* of a grenade flying through the air signaled the ambush.

"Dammit!" Troy shouted.

Simon dropped behind cover as the grenade beeped. He searched the ground for the threat as the shrill tone warned him of its impending detonation.

"I think it's stuck on me," Tucker said quietly, looking grim. He appeared small in the middle of the dirt path, holding his newfound weapon and staring at it forlornly. "I didn't even get to fire it."

The beeping reached the height of its intensity, and their rookie disappeared into a ball of fire. Simon swore out loud.

"It's a trap!" Collins called out. "Get to the Citadel! Now!"

He and Troy hurried toward the white tower in the distance at full speed. Troy didn't even glance back to the black smudge marring the ground where his brother had stood moments before.

Tucker's last words echoed in Simon's head. A shiny new weapon—it was classic bait, and their most naïve squad member had fallen for it.

Simon was shuffling to follow the departing forms of his teammates when his visor dinged. Malachi was wounded.

"They went wide," he said weakly. "I'm down."

Simon whipped around toward Malachi's vantage point. "I'm on my way!"

"Negative! The Citadel is the waypoint, Simon," Collins barked. "We'll need you to capture it."

"I can save him!" Simon cried out, already a quarter of the way back to the rooftop where Malachi had set up shop. He dodged around the familiar layout of the crumbling courtyard. He just needed a second to get back.

"Get back here!" Troy said through the com. Collins's fury had devolved into unintelligible shouts at their incompetence.

"You're not going to make it, Simon," Malachi said. "They got me good, and I think my time is running out."

"Don't say that! I can do this!" He tossed his gun on his back so he could run faster up the weathered stairs that led out of the maze of stone walls. "I'm almost there!"

"You guys will be okay without me," Malachi said. "I think I can hear my mother calling." His voice was faint and far away.

The building was up ahead. He was going to make it. Simon would get him back on his feet, and they would catch up with the others at the Citadel.

His helmet dinged. He stopped in his tracks.

Malachi was dead.

Simon gulped and took a second to collect himself, absorbing his *failure*. He cast a wary look at the HUD on his visor. A red dot on the radar was rapidly approaching. He pivoted quickly, shooting from the hip as the Draconian soldier came around the corner, silver blade drawn and poised.

His submachine gun recoiled violently, spattering reckless bullet holes over the stone wall and into the pasty gray form of the enemy. It wasn't a great tactic as far as accuracy went, but at least *he* was still alive. The light dimmed in the nameless Draconian's inhuman yellow eyes.

He could hear gunfire in the distance. He shook his head and dashed up the middle of the courtyard toward the Citadel. There was no time for stealth in his approach.

"I didn't get to Malachi in time," he told them over the com, his footfalls echoing steadily in the weaving corridors.

"No shit," Collins said. "We're under heavy fire, Simon, and guess what? *You're not here!*"

After a burst from Troy's Death Machine, an indicator on his display blinked out of existence.

Troy cheered loudly.

"Any eyes on the other ones?" Simon asked as he slowed and crouched behind cover, poking his head out to survey the base of the Citadel. Collins and Troy were huddled up behind an old altar. Troy was threading an ammunition belt into his heavy weapon as Collins laid down fire to keep the invaders behind cover.

"Two are pinned down," Collins said, his temper in check for the moment. "They have a sniper somewhere out there. I can hear the rifle firing. Keep your head out of the line of sight unless you want to be eight pounds lighter."

"Best diet in the Arcadian Army," Troy quipped.

Simon grinned. They had lost a lot today, but it would be okay. They would get through this battle and eventually, when his luck ran out, *he would see his friends again.*

"Death Machine's ready. Throw your 'nade, commander." Troy heaved his large weapon off the ground, arms straining under the weight. Collins ducked behind cover to pull the pin from his grenade. He popped back out, hurled the projectile, and then dropped back behind the altar.

As predicted, the Draconians shouted, warnings spilling from their helmets in a foreign tongue, and ran forward to escape the boom of the grenade. A shrill hiss, like a kettle on the verge of explosion, preceded the continuous fire from Troy's heavy machine gun.

The Draconians fell.

Simon grinned widely.

"*Finally!*" Collins shouted. "The Citadel is ours!"

"All right, gentlemen," Troy said smoothly as he turned toward the looming structure, "I think I deserve the honor of opening the doors. After all, I got *three* of them."

"Excuse me?" Collins said, sounding scandalized. "I guess you forgot about my daring heroics last Thursday."

Troy chuckled. "Pardon my poor memory. Must be from all the killin'." He tossed the strap to his heavy gun over his head and let it hang from his back.

"What do you think is in there?" Simon craned his head back to look up at the stone obelisk stretching into the sky. The sight made his stomach turn, and he crossed his arms. Months of missions had gone into storming the Citadel, filled with battles, bloodshed, and hours laughing with his friends. He wished Tucker and Malachi could be here to see what was inside of it.

Troy pushed on one of the large stone doors as the few remaining members of the Knights looked on in awed silence.

The booming shot of a sniper rifle ripped through the air, sparking adrenaline in Simon's veins. Troy's outstretched palms slid along the stone before his knees hit the ground.

"Medic!" Collins cried out. "Hurry! Revive him, Simon!"

The sniper. How did they forget about him?

Every moment felt like an eternity as he heard the bolt handle reset, spitting out the hot empty cartridge. It fell out of the chamber and onto the gravel. Simon barely had a moment to duck into one of the corridors surrounding the Citadel before the gun fired again.

"I can't revive a head wound, Collins. I can't save him," Simon said into the radio.

The com line was quiet. A glance at his HUD told him everything he needed to know.

He was alone.

That second shot—he hadn't been its target.

His hands shook as panic finally took hold of him.

He could hear the crunch of boots on gravel. He checked his gun and reloaded while safely tucked behind cover. Metal shifted, and something heavy thumped as it fell to the ground.

A sharp whistle—that same familiar buildup from Troy's Death Machine—rang out, and the gleaming smile of a lone Draconian flashed before Simon was cut in half.

DEFEATED appeared in large red letters on his ComSphere visor.

"No!" Simon raged, slamming his palms into the arms of his desk chair.

The score was tallied, and the game lobby appeared.

"Well—" Tucker started.

"Don't," Troy said.

"—at least we got further than last time."

Simon shook his head and unclipped the front display of his visor before turning the volume down on his headset.

"What kind of *idiot* thinks they're just going to find a Draconian weapon lying in the dirt?" Collins shouted. Simon could hear something being hurled across the room four hundred miles away in Richmond.

"I can't believe we forgot about the sniper. I feel like such a noob," Simon grumbled.

"You outlived me." Malachi laughed. "Thanks for the attempted save, by the way."

"You can thank me next time when I *actually save you*," Simon said wryly.

"It's cool though. My mom came in and made me fold my laundry. So, it's not like I could have played anyway."

"Can we try again?" Tucker asked, upbeat as always.

Simon glanced down at his battery. "I only have ten minutes left. Gotta recharge soon."

"Pitiful." Collins must have finished his tantrum. The guy was an ass, but Simon had known him and Troy since Arcadian Fortress II.

They had met at the Annual Northeast Regional PlayerCon Qualifier and co-oped together through two iterations of the game. They met Malachi at the con a few years later. Their fifth had come and gone, and then Troy had started inviting his younger brother into the fold.

Tucker sighed in relief. "Good! I've had to pee for like an hour. Talk to you guys tomorrow!" He didn't wait for anyone to say goodbye before he dropped his headset on his desk with a thunk, making the others wince. When he logged out, Tucker's online handle vanished from the holoscreen display on the gauntlet strapped to Simon's left arm.

"We only played the level once, Simon. What's up with your rig?" Collins asked.

"I have two panels charging my reserves all day, but I can't use all my batteries for this," Simon said, his face warming. It was hard to talk to a chatroom full of gamers about playing fewer video games. "I don't know how it is where you guys are, but it's getting bad here."

"There have been riots in Charlotte," Troy said quietly. "Some people came through town and told us about it. I thought for sure the rations would be better if you lived in a city, but from the way they looked, they're getting almost nothing. Skin and bones, you know?"

"What about you and Tucker? Your family. Are you guys okay?" Simon hated to pry, but he had been friends with Troy for seven years.

"We're fine. Gastonia has a lot of farmland. We'll survive."

Simon stayed quiet and watched the circular holoscreen display as another percent ticked off his battery. "Did you guys get into the maintenance records last night?" he asked hopefully.

"Can't you get in trouble for accessing government databases? I mean—UNID, they send people to prison for this stuff, right?" Troy asked.

"To get caught by the UN's Investigation Department, you have to be intercepted by their cybersecurity or leave footprints that set off red flags," Malachi said. "Luckily for us, they either can't do their jobs without the grid, or they don't think anyone else can hack in without it, so they're not even trying to stop us."

"So, you got in?" Simon took his glasses off and rubbed his eyes, stretching.

Collins sighed. "Yes, but let's just take a second before—"

Malachi laughed humorlessly. "I knew it! I knew you were going to pretend like—"

"Guys! I only have a few minutes. Just tell me!" Simon snapped. "The manufacturer's records were a bust. Again." He had spent most of the night—of the week, really—trying to gain access into GlassStar Labs' server, but every countermeasure he broke through had another locked vault behind it. He needed some good news.

Collins finally relented. "We got in, and I don't know what we were really expecting. I mean, if there were no new records on the grid repair then that could mean no one is working on fixing it, or it could mean they can't store records on their satellite server anymore because *the grid is down*. Honestly, that's what I figured we'd find, and then we'd have to listen to Malachi bitch about the government for a few more years."

Troy chuckled. "Here we go."

"Your small, closed-off little brain can't handle that Big Brother might not be completely on the up-and-up, can it?" Malachi said. "We saw it at Roswell. That's completely been one hundred percent proven as a fact—"

"Roswell?" Collins repeated incredulously. "There was never a UFO! You're crazy. It was a spy plane. It was always a stealth ship. The Air Force admitted that shit *decades ago*."

"Oh yeah? And JFK?" Malachi countered.

"I am not talking to you about JFK again, Malachi," Collins spat.

"Did you watch the videos? I sent you links—did you even click them?"

Simon winced as Malachi's tone became shrill.

"Guys!" Simon yelled. "What did you see?"

Malachi got his crazy back in order and returned from his tangent. "There were *a lot* of new records, but we think they were concentrated in one part of the country. The IPs that logged them were similar. I'm going to figure out the where tonight."

"All right, that's a little weird, I guess. But what were they working on?" Simon prodded.

"It took a while to get past their standard security measures," Collins said. "We didn't get to dig deep. I needed to break through their encryption, but that was going to take time we didn't have. You never want to stay somewhere you're not supposed to be for longer than you have to. I'm going to get back into their database tonight by myself while Mal does his thing."

"Good work, guys," Simon said. "I really couldn't do any of this without your help."

"Yeah, yeah," Collins replied with an air of disinterest. "Just remember to not get your hopes up, Si."

Simon felt uncomfortable. There was mixed support from his friends on his work. Something was going on that the government knew about. There was something they weren't telling anyone, and Simon was determined to get to the bottom of it. People were suffering, and he was going to help them.

Malachi was on his side, but then again Malachi had always been a little crazy. Simon believed in his grid theory in the very marrow of his bones. Hearing it compared to Roswell and Kennedy's untimely end made him wonder if he had spent a few too many hours listening to Malachi's spiel. Maybe *he'd* gone crazy, too.

Collins didn't buy into Simon's theory at all. Simon had taken a little heat from him over the past few weeks. Not playing the game was blasphemy in Collins's eyes. Admittedly, before the power grid failed, Simon wouldn't have even considered abandoning his Arcadian squad for something in the *real* world.

This was different though. This was serious. This could be permanent, and Simon was going to do his best to prevent that. Collins was sharp as a tack. Asking for his help to get behind sophisticated encryption and fortified firewalls meant Simon needed to keep him happy, and keeping Collins happy meant being a team player in Arcadian Fortress V.

He hated having to hide his continued use of the game from his twin, though. West wouldn't understand.

"Oh yeah, and thank you for your moral support, Troy." Simon grinned.

Troy snorted. "Look, in Arcadia, I'm a god. Three kills in one match," he reminded them. Troy rarely took a position on the grid theory—actually, Troy rarely took a position on anything. Troy was Switzerland.

"I'm at three percent," Simon said. "Gotta shut down my ComSphere before it dies and corrupts something I need. I'll see you guys tomorrow night."

"Tomorrow, we take the Citadel," Collins replied, his tone full of determination and authority. "Oh, and Simon?"

"Yeah?"

"Real quick, before you go—I thought about your charging issues. Are you still using those cheap cables from the Supercenter?" Simon could hear Collins typing, his taps on his keyboard sounding like an automatic weapon.

"Yeah, why?"

"It's probably a problem with the wires. I'd switch them out if I were you."

"Will do, commander." Simon smiled before logging out and shutting his rig down. His gauntlet's holoscreen flickered off, and the basement was shrouded in darkness.

He had never really known what it meant to be in total darkness. There'd always been something blinking, the clock on the microwave or the flash of his brother's cell phone while he was texting some girl in the middle of the night.

He leaned his head back in his chair and sighed. *Time to get to work.*

He flipped the small lamp he had rigged to run on some of the extra power he was gathering from his solar panels and then removed the gauntlet from his wrist. He removed the solar cell and carefully cleaned the connections before spot-checking for corrosion. The batteries were supposed to be changed out after a few hundred recharges but finding them was proving to be difficult.

The ComSphere.

When he'd first heard of its upcoming release two years ago, he had stared incredulously at his dual monitors and immediately dialed Collins.

A console that ran on solar panels? That only held an hour or two of charge at a time? It was impractical and almost insulting. The makers of ComSphere wanted players to leave their comfort zones. He hadn't wanted the system, had loathed the idea of the forced activity. Executives looking down from their top floor offices, judging him, judging his friends. The whole premise of the console was a corporation's attempt to correct gamers who were *broken* by their obsessions, forced into a life of introversion and heart disease.

For longer play times, you needed to recharge the batteries in the daylight. If you wanted the best loot, you could use the GPS capabilities of the system and follow waypoints in the distance. Walk a mile, and you get an upgrade on your health. Two miles would get you a new gun. Five would unlock special abilities like quick firing and heavier armor.

It all boiled down to one main objective: to force gamers to go outside.

Simon gathered up his spare solar panels, his neatly arranged cables, and the extra batteries he had scrimped to afford and trudged up the stairs of his parents' house as the early light of the morning peeked in through the small basement window.

He sidestepped West's backpack in the hallway, glaring at it. It had been there for three weeks, and it didn't seem like West planned on moving it anytime soon.

Last June, the late-night trash talk between Simon and his friends about the console had reached its peak in the stratosphere before plummeting the eleven miles back down to Earth. The release details of Arcadian Fortress V had come out, and it was going to be a ComSphere exclusive.

Collins had raged for hours while they price-checked the system and cast a more critical eye at its specs. They came up with a way to get around the forced activity requirements. Multiple charge stations and the constant cycling of backup batteries would make the one to two hours of daily play time extend to whatever they needed.

It was an expensive endeavor up front, but Arcadian Fortress had been a central part of his life for years. The game had always been his connection with his friends and an escape from himself when his mind got too loud. Whenever someone at school made him feel like the weird quiet kid and whenever he got into a disagreement with his twin, Arcadian Fortress was there for him. ComSphere exclusive or not, he had known he wasn't giving up on the series.

And now Simon owed *everything* to the console he hadn't even wanted. The purchase of this system meant he was one of the few people in his small town who still had power after the collapse of the grid. As long as the satellites providing internet stayed in the sky, he could still be connected.

He yawned and breathed in the morning air. His eyes were bleary behind his reading glasses, and he could barely make out the wide stretches of his parents' farmland. On autopilot, he walked around the house and behind the privacy fence. He sat his supplies carefully on the ground and began setting up for the day. He needed every drop of sunshine to meet his energy needs. That meant being up at daybreak every single morning.

He cautiously unfolded the large arrays of solar panels, loaded the battery station, and secured the connections with his cheap wires. He'd have to figure out a way to sneak off sometime soon to replace them. If he could charge faster, he could get more things working in the house for his parents while still maintaining his workload.

Although the ComSphere had its own built-in panels, they were clunky, small, and not as impressive as the replacement units Collins had recommended. He could charge more batteries at once if he used the ComSphere as it was intended, but he didn't want to risk the console getting wet outside. After all, the only weather report he had been receiving came in the form of his mother's hip pain flaring up, and she didn't always let him know ahead of time. The designers had thought of this, of course, but there was a reason why the box the ComSphere came in had said water-resistant instead of waterproof.

No, using the spare units was a less risky plan.

Once everything was set up correctly, he stumbled back into the house. He ignored the rumble in his stomach and padded back down to the basement.

He was dead on his feet after being up all night sneaking around GlassStar Labs' satellite server, picking open virtual locks and making halfhearted, unnecessary attempts at covering his tracks. His mother would wake him up in two hours, and then he could cycle his charging station. She hated it when he slept into the afternoon.

WEST

HE LOVED THIS PART of the day. Alone, with just his thoughts for company, patiently waiting for supper to take the bait under the smooth surface of the water. He'd been fishing on this lake for as long as he could remember. It was a short walk from his family's farm, backing up to their eastern cornfields. He never really cared about farming, not like his dad, but he did like the open spaces with no civilization in sight.

But now, even his time on the lakeshore was losing appeal. This used to be his escape from reality. Now it *was* reality. He felt an enormous amount of pressure to bring something home every day. Three months had passed since the lights went out, and Lake Jocassee was showing serious signs of overharvesting.

With that depressing thought, West rolled his shoulders. He'd been sitting in the same position for two hours with nothing to show for his efforts. He'd been lucky yesterday with a good take, but his luck wouldn't last forever. They were avoiding using their generators for anything other than an emergency, and refrigeration had quickly become a luxury they couldn't afford. Fresh was key right now.

Standing up, he stretched out kinks and began to gather his meager supplies. Suddenly, his bobber made a quick duck under the water. He lunged for his pole and pulled up sharply before reeling in the line.

Shouting in triumph, he heaved out a smallmouth bass the size of his forearm. Maybe tomorrow would be different, but for today his luck was holding out. After tossing his catch into a bucket, he picked up the rest of his gear and began to walk back to the house.

It was another hot Carolina summer, but he guessed the power could have gone out at a worse time. He and his twin brother Simon had just graduated high school when everything went to hell. He should have started spring football training last week at South Carolina, and Simon should be getting ready to start at MIT. But now? Everything was on hold. Who knew when normal things like sports and school would begin again?

He mounted the stairs to the back porch, lost in thought. He noticed his mother sitting in the kitchen window seat. Through the glass of the large window, he could see the worry in her eyes. That was all she did these days.

"Hey, Mom," he said, entering through the back door. "Dinner is served." He lowered the bucket to the floor.

His mom grinned, though it didn't manage to reach her eyes. The struggle to stay positive right now was real. But he refused to let his concerns show. He hadn't told them yet that the lake's supply was getting low, and he was hoping like hell he wouldn't have to. The UN needed to figure this mess out, and quick.

West hadn't seen Simon out of the basement in days. He was obsessed with finding the source of the outage, and he seemed to think that with enough digging, he could *save the world*. But honestly, if anyone could accomplish such a feat, it might be his brother. West would never admit it out loud, but Simon was a genius—with computers, at least. Everything else, not so much.

"West," his mom said, "your dad and I are leaving right after dinner tonight. I'll need you and Simon to run into town for your father's prescriptions."

Now, that was unexpected. His parents hated for them to go into town. It was only allowed these days if they went together. He guessed his dad's meds must be running low if they were asking the two of them to make a trip so late in the day.

"Why the rush if you'll be gone by the time we get back?" His parents had been planning this trip to the state-sponsored farmers market to set up a booth for a while. They'd be gone at least a week.

"He's not running low just yet," she said. "He has about sixty doses left, but, I heard from Mrs. Oslo down the street today that the pharmacy hasn't had a new shipment in a while. I'm worried if we don't act now, there may not be any left by the time we get back."

West could tell from her expression she was downplaying her concern. Their funds, like everyone else's, were depleting at an alarming rate, but it wasn't like his dad could live without his meds. He was diabetic, and not only did he need regular insulin injections, but he also needed a better diet than their meager stores were supplying. At least their portable cooler ran on batteries and kept what they had cold. Without that, he'd probably be dead already.

Everyone but Simon sat at the table to eat dinner. Simon got a plate delivered downstairs. After cleaning up his mess, West headed to the door that led to the basement. Simon wasn't going to like being pulled away from his computer, but he'd get over it.

He knocked once, then poked his head into the dark stairwell. "Hey, Si," he called down. "We have to make a trip into town. Parents' orders."

West could hear the deep sigh all the way up the stairs.

"I really don't have time for this. A trip to town will take hours!" Simon shouted.

"Tough. We gotta get Dad's shots, and we need to get there before they close." West frowned. "So, hustle up."

Simon's footsteps got louder as he plodded up the stairs.

"Let me get my shoes," he said once he reached the landing.

West gave Simon a glance, wondering how it was possible they were twins. He was wearing a T-shirt that said, 'There's no place like 127.0.0.1.' West had no idea what that meant, but Simon was always wearing things that made no sense to him.

"You want to be single forever, don't you?" he asked Simon, pointing to the shirt.

Simon rolled his eyes. "Some of us aren't man-whores...and I like this shirt."

"So that's a yes to the single life then."

"Shut up," he snapped. "Let's get this over with. The sooner we leave, the sooner I can get back to work."

Simon turned the corner and came back into view, kicking over West's pack in his haste to leave.

"Watch where you're going, Si!" West picked it back up, then headed to his parents' office to grab some cash from the safe.

"Well, it's right in the middle of the floor," Simon grumbled.

Simon's things were precious and off-limits. West's were apparently garbage.

The two of them set out on a trail that would take them to the main road and into town. It was four miles. That used to take them all of five minutes to travel in a car, but now it meant over an hour.

As they walked, West wondered what his friends were up to. Summer used to be full of days doing nothing but hanging out, swimming, and parties. They still got together about once a week, but coordinating these things was almost impossible now. If you didn't have a standing appointment, you were out of luck. *Maybe we should learn Morse code, or smoke signals or something.*

Next week's party would be at Leah's house. He wasn't sure if he would be going. She didn't want to see him, and he didn't have time for her drama.

"Do you mind if we stop by TechCenter on our way back?" Simon asked, interrupting his thoughts.

"I don't know if that's a good idea, Si. People are going to start getting suspicious if you keep going in there. People don't need tech if they don't have power." He emphasized his point with raised eyebrows.

"Yes, but *I* have power, and I need new cables. I'm not getting the charge out of my panels they should be generating. I think the lines are old and causing a dirty connection to the—"

"Shh! What the hell, Simon? Are you looking to start a riot in our front yard?"

"There isn't anyone around to hear me," Simon hissed.

"You never know! The last thing we need is someone overhearing you, and it getting around."

Simon sighed. "I know, you're right. It's not like we can even power our appliances though. I need everything I have to work on the outage. We're getting so close. Collins found the UN maintenance logs. The evidence is really piling up, and I think if I just have a little more time..."

West listened with one ear as Simon droned on. His brother might be smart, but was he smarter than the entire UN? Was it realistic to expect he could fix this from their parents' basement when government experts around the world couldn't?

"Look," he said, breaking into the conversation as soon as Simon took a breath, "I get what you are doing is super important." He rolled his eyes dramatically to indicate how likely he thought that was. "But you still need to be cautious."

"No worries, I will," Simon promised, crossing his heart in sarcasm. "I still need to make that stop at the store. We'll be discreet."

"Discreet? You think this body can be discreet? If there are women around, I can't make any promises."

"That's ridiculous. We have the same body," Simon protested.

"No, *that's* ridiculous. My body looks like I care, and yours looks like it's been moldering in a basement."

Simon seemed to contemplate this.

"Do you really think I look bad?" he asked a little self-consciously. He looked down his front and inspected himself.

West took a closer look at his brother. Same sandy blond hair, same six-foot height, and the same brown eyes. To the casual onlooker, there were very few noticeable differences. Simon usually wore his reading glasses, which West wouldn't be caught dead in. Anyone could tell West had spent some time in the weight room. He'd been bulking up for football season. But the biggest difference was the way Simon seemed to carry the weight of the world on his shoulders. He always looked a little haggard.

"Honestly, you could use some time in the sun," West told him straight-faced. Simon's eyes narrowed, and West burst out laughing, barely dodging a high tree root as he walked. "Dude, you look fine. You're at least half as hot as me, and that's still saying something."

"This conversation is over," he grumbled.

A few more minutes, and they finally crossed the gravel path leading to the main road.

Their walk into town had passed quickly. The sun was just dipping below the horizon, and the pharmacy would still be open for at least another twenty minutes.

The town was already showing signs of deterioration. Aside from the obvious lack of light down the main thoroughfare, graffiti was creeping onto many of the buildings. Most of the cars sat pushed to the side of the road with flat tires and broken windows. Too many dumb kids with nothing to occupy their time but vandalism.

That said, defacing the billboards was a pastime he could get behind. Slogans like "Camden Can" or "Camden/Gamble 2059" were all over the place. At least eighty percent of the town's signage had been bought by the Camden campaign when the grid first went live.

They'd boasted incessantly about the success of the Global Power Project. Cities across the country immediately dismantled their existing grids for recycling. *What a bunch of well-intentioned idiots.* And all that advertising meant everyone knew exactly who to blame when the whole world stopped.

Many people in town had made a hobby of vandalizing the politician's likeness. He'd taken a couple of tomatoes to that smug face himself before he'd realized how precious every bite of food would be in just a few short weeks.

As they turned the corner, he spied the black tower that cast a shadow over the town. It was a tall waste of new age tech. Everyone had cheered the day they completed construction. It was one step closer to power that would never fail—until it did. Now it was just a useless but poignant reminder of everyone's stupidity.

Every time they entered town, it seemed a little less safe. Most of the store owners still showed up and opened their businesses like clockwork. Maybe they were hopeful the lights would one day flip back on. Or maybe they just didn't have anything else to do. But most likely they were afraid that if they didn't show up, shotgun in hand, they wouldn't have a store worth coming back to once it did come on again.

"Why don't we split up? You can grab your cables and whatnot, and I'll pick up Dad's prescription. We can meet back in front of Billy's tire shop." The habit of making plans like this ahead of time instead of simply texting one's location still felt strange to him.

"You know Mom and Dad don't like us splitting up," Simon replied, looking around anxiously.

"Yeah, but I also know you want to get back to your research as fast as possible," he reasoned back to him, knowing the temptation to make this trip quick would overrule his desire to follow orders.

"Fine, but let's both be fast about it. I don't want word to get back to them that we weren't together."

West gave him a jaunty salute and strode toward the pharmacy. He liked to chat up the girl who worked behind the counter, and he didn't need Simon's awkwardness messing with his game.

As he strode in, he allowed his gaze to fall on Marcie Benton. She was about to be a senior, and he could tell she was into him. Every time he stopped in, she blushed like crazy. Already he could see the flush moving up her face as he approached her counter.

"Wow, Marcie, did you do something different with your hair?" he asked. It looked the same as it always did to him, but he figured girls were always doing something different with their hair, so odds were she'd say yes.

"I can't believe you noticed." She giggled, then smiled broadly in his direction.

Yep, nailed it.

"How can I help you?" Marcie asked, breathlessly.

"I need a refill on my dad's prescription," he said, handing over the small wad of cash he knew should cover it, "and I need to take you out on Saturday night. What time will you be getting off work?"

Her grin grew even wider, if that was possible, but faded just as quickly.

"Oh, your dad's prescription...you see, we didn't get any new shipments after his last refill. I'm not sure when we'll be getting a new one in, you know?" She bit her lip uncertainly, checking for his reaction.

It was all he could do not to throw his fist into the leaflet stand nearby.

Damn. This is not good. His mom had been right, but it was too late. Maybe other towns would have something, but if the local pharmacy had been out since his last refill...that was four weeks ago. No one would have insulin at this point.

He was going to hyperventilate if he didn't get out of this store. Dazed, he walked back out, barely remembering to pick up the cash he'd set on the counter.

"About that date..." he heard her say behind him, but he didn't stop. He couldn't think about a date with a girl who giggled over nothing while his dad could be dying.

Looking around, he tried to remember where he should be meeting his brother. He was just recalling that he'd be at Billy's when a shout rang out down the street.

It was never a good idea these days to follow noises like that. Even in a small town where people knew each other, they were not the same kindhearted people they used to be. However, he was sure that had been his brother's shout.

Just when he'd started moving toward Simon's voice, the distinct sound of a gunshot rang out. He burst into motion, pumping his legs as fast as he could in the direction of the shot. When he rounded the corner behind the tech shop, he saw a dark lump huddled on the ground, and he skidded to a stop.

SIMON

THERE WAS A TIME WHEN going into tech stores had filled Simon's heart with joy; they were some of the few brick-and-mortar establishments he felt at ease in. It had been comforting to have a place that didn't make him want to find a nice quiet corner to hide in until it was acceptable to leave.

But that had all been taken away from him. West had been right—buying new cables was risky. If the wrong person saw him make the purchase, then people might find out about his solar rig.

He'd heard of people getting mugged for goods recently, a side effect of distribution lines vanishing and store shelves being empty. If they were willing to steal things like shoes and paperback books, he could only imagine what they would do if they found out he had access to the scarcest resource on the planet—electricity.

It was for this reason Simon ducked into the alley beside the TechCenter. He'd enter through the back door, make up some lie to satisfy the owner's curiosity, and leave the way he came.

He stood in the deserted alley, which was barely lit by the setting sun, and took a second to psych himself up for the story he was about to weave.

He hated the unease that came before interacting face-to-face with people outside of his family. He hated the loud echoing in his mind, and he hated that he couldn't just *live*. He couldn't stay out of his head and be in the moment because of the suffocating what-ifs rattling around. Everything came so easy for West, but for Simon, every moment out of the basement was a struggle. Life in Arcadia was easier.

Simon pushed down the panic and reached to pull open the heavy steel door. Quick footfalls bounced off brick walls as a figure came around the corner and barreled into him.

"Hey!" Simon yelled, falling hard on the concrete. The man, eyes wide and frantic, paid him no mind before jumping to his feet with surprising spryness and booking it further into the alleyway.

Before Simon could scramble up off the ground, a deafening shot rang out. With the swiftness of a switch being flipped, Simon's mind shifted from loud, cluttered unease into sharp focus. He felt a sick sense of familiarity as the man crumpled to a heap, holding his side and groaning.

Without thought, Simon rushed over to him.

There was blood. It was pooling up under him and soaking through his shirt. Sticky red stained the white concrete. The man was holding his wound weakly with one hand, and the other was clutched tightly into a fist. Simon moved the man's hand aside and applied steady pressure with his own.

"I'm going to get you help, okay? Everything will be fine," he said firmly. "What's your name?"

His face was pale, eyes watery and fearful as he met Simon's gaze. "Martin," he rasped before coughing violently.

"It's all going to be okay, Martin," Simon assured him again. The calmness took hold of him. He turned to call out to the road. He could hold his position while someone else ran to get help. There was a fire station up the street, and someone there would know how to handle the wound until they could get Martin to emergency care.

Before he could open his mouth, a bony hand clutched his wrist. "Don't!" Martin wheezed. "You need to go. Leave me here and go."

Simon shook his head. "No way."

"You need to run," Martin hissed, "before they get you, too."

Simon's eyes widened as the gravity of the situation solidified. "Who did this to you? Why?" His words were quick-fire, low and measured.

Martin coughed and then smiled weakly. His teeth were stained with blood. "I sold my soul to the devil—had no idea the hell we would bring when the grid fell." He laughed bitterly, and angry tears ran down his cheeks as his breathing became shallow.

Simon's red hands pulled back at Martin's confession.

"I'm so sorry." Martin wept, body quaking as systems failed. "Please forgive me. I thought if I could find him—"

Heavy footfalls behind them made Simon whip around.

"What the hell is going on?"

"Shut up, West! I can't hear him," Simon snapped. He set his jaw, turned his attention back to the dying man and again put pressure on the wound with steady hands. But the blood kept flowing, and he realized he couldn't save this man. Very soon, Martin would be dead.

Martin's eyes were filled with regret. "I failed everyone—I know that, but there's a man who can fix it. He's somewhere in this town. Goes by the handle SI-FIGHTER. He'll know what to do." He clutched Simon's wrist like a lifeline.

Martin reached his other hand, the one that had been clenched in a fist, toward Simon. He opened his palm and offered him something.

It was a nano-drive, and he seemed to believe it was worth dying for.

"Waypoint." Martin paused, fighting his body as it shut down. "Find Waypoint."

Need to know what happens next?
Click here[1] to find out!

---

1. http://books2read.com/adamsperkins-waypoint

INTEL: A WAYPOINT PREQUEL NOVELLA

Never miss an update by joining our mailing list[2]!

---

2. http://eepurl.com/dCvo6r

About the Authors

DEBORAH ADAMS AND KIMBERLEY PERKINS are friends and coworkers. They share a love of coffee, literature, and teenagers saving the world. By day, they work for a defense contractor in Huntsville, Alabama as the HR Director and an Excel-wielding Analyst, respectively. By night, they build worlds with words and devour stories. For more information about Deborah Adams and Kimberley Perkins and their foray into writing, check them out on social media.

Twitter:
@DebAdams_Writer and @Kim_Writes
Facebook:
@authordeborahadams and @kimberleywrites
Youtube: Adams / Perkins

www.ingramcontent.com/pod-product-compliance
Lightning Source LLC
Chambersburg PA
CBHW030537130626
46552CB00006B/2301